Crackroaches

GARY LEE VINCENT

Crackroaches
By **Gary Lee Vincent**

Burning Bulb Publishing
P.O. Box 4721
Bridgeport, WV 26330-4721
United States of America
www.BurningBulbPublishing.com

Cover designed by Max Cave as a work for hire between Fuzzy Monkey Films and Burning Bulb Publishing. Artwork © 2024 and used with permission of respective studios.

First Edition.

Paperback Edition ISBN: 978-1-964172-03-3

Also by Gary Lee Vincent

Novels
PASSAGEWAY
BELLY TIMBER
ATTACK OF THE MELONHEADS
WHEN THE BEDPOSTS SHAKE (RING OF THE SUCCUBUS)
IMPOUND
STRANGE FRIENDS
THE BEST ACTORS THAT EVER LIVED
JEROME
THE BLIND MELODY

Darkened—The West Virginia Vampire Series
DARKENED HILLS
DARKENED HOLLOWS
DARKENED WATERS
DARKENED SOULS
DARKENED MINDS
DARKENED DESTINIES

The Douglas River Vampire Series
RIVER: A VAMPIRE'S NIGHTMARE
ICARUS

The Crackimals Series
CRACKCOON
CRACKODILE
CRACKSQUATCH
CRACKROACHES

The Black Circle Chronicles
PROVE YOUR LOVE
STRANGE NEW POWERS
NIGHT WINGS
SHEEP AMONGST WOLVES
LORD OF THE BIRDS

Nonfiction
THE WINNER, THE LOSER
AGELATIONS
CONFIGURATION MANAGEMENT

Musical Releases
100 PERCENT
PASSION, PLEASURE, & PAIN
SOMEWHERE DOWN THE ROAD

Dedicated to
Rich Bottles Jr.

CHAPTER 1

The Futures Bioresearch facility lay in the woods on the outskirts of the West Virginian town of Huttonsville.

The facility consisted of a large complex of buildings. Because of its situation near the Appalachian Mountains with its forests and wildlife (not to mention the perpetual problem of nosy campers from the nearby campground and overly inquisitive bears rooting through the trash for lunch or dinner), the Futures facility was surrounded by a chain-link fence.

Businesswise, Futures Bioresearch ('F-Bio' for short) mostly handled contracts for medical and pharmaceutical companies. The latter area of contracting had resulted in them doing some work for the US Government, including, in some cases, the local police.

One such case was being handled now in Lab 7, the last laboratory in one of the research facility's rear blocks.

Lab 7 was Dr. Annabelle Cole's lab, and she and her assistant, Doyle Sanders, were currently working with the West Virginian police to determine the specific narcotic properties of that extremely addictive variant of crack cocaine known as Agent Orange.

***

Dr. Cole frowned at the latest results on her PC tablet.

How the hell did that guy Max ever manage this? The guy was an evil genius!

Despite her revulsion at what the late Max Carillo had created during his short adult lifetime, Annabelle Cole couldn't help but feel admiration for the dead chemist.

Though still only vaguely understood—F-Bio had gotten the contract just a week ago—what Annabelle and Doyle had so far been able to determine about Agent Orange was scary.

It's like a highway trip to hell wired directly to the brain. Like the flick Total Recall, but without Arnie and full of those Martian freaks instead!

***

Dr. Cole was a short brunette. A long time ago she'd been young and hot, but a life dedicated to study—too much study in everyone's opinion except hers—had etched deep ruts in her face, even as the normal aging process had turned her hair gray and leeched her strength.

Back then too, she'd had a family. A husband and a daughter. But the husband was long gone, a victim, he claimed, of his wife's overly studious nature.

Annabelle felt Joseph Cole simply couldn't keep his dick in his pants. A husband was supposed to have some consideration for his wife, and Joe Cole clearly hadn't had any for her. Truth be told, she felt she was better off without him; once science called, meeting the needs of another person and handling the duties of marriage had never been a priority to her, just a messy set of encumbrances in the former case and a waste of valuable research time in the latter.

She and Joe's daughter Jenny was all grown up now, but she visited sometimes from college, where she was studying to be a biochemist like her mother. So, her life had more or less worked itself out in the end.

***

Annabelle Cole studied the results again; scrolled down, then up, then down once more. Then she turned to stare at the rodents the tests had come from. These were all securely locked in cages that were just as securely secured to the laboratory walls. As a further assurance of security, each of the little animals in those cages had a flexible metal band (like a segmented metal wristwatch strap) around its middle; this band sufficiently tightened to ensure that the animal it restrained would be unable to slip either its haunches or shoulders through it.

To the casual observer, such a level of security for rats and rabbits would seem like overkill; merely further evidence to ban animal testing.

Annabelle Cole shuddered. She, too, had felt similarly at first. But then the police scientists who'd brought her the Agent Orange samples had shown her a few videos recorded in Max Carillo's lab at the time of his death. After watching those videos, Annabelle had had no further reservations. Seeing Max's dead girlfriend with rats and rabbits crawling their way through holes in her body—while still eating her— had almost made her throw up.

She stared at the caged rats and rabbits, all of whom stared back at her with unblinking orange eyes—eyes that were all that selfsame solid color, like giant misplaced LEDs—eyes that projected anger and hunger; or hunger and anger at the watcher. Annabelle wasn't sure which instinct was higher in her little test subjects.

The constant they all shared was the urge to commit violence. This was visible in the way the rodents strained at their leashes from time to time, the muscle groupings beneath their fur visibly bunching up with their desire and tension. Several of the restrained animals gnawed at the unbreakable metal links with such fervor that they split their hairy lips and chipped their own teeth. Then, still not willing to accept defeat, they licked up their own blood and hissed at Annabelle and Doyle.

Here was another puzzle: how the carnivorous element in the rats' omnivorous nature had seemingly gained the ascendency. Of course, the puzzle was stranger where the rabbits were concerned, as it required explaining how a genetic herbivore suddenly turned carnivore overnight.

And all that was caused by this, Annabelle thought glumly, picking up a piece of Agent Orange from the small transparent package of the drug that lay near her lab instruments. *It looks so much like candy that I could pop it into my mouth without thinking.*

And that was a scary thought. Because Dr. Annabelle Cole knew how addictive Agent Orange was. Not just from staring at her captive orange-eyed rats either. To understand how dangerous this new street drug was, she'd visited a morgue where the corpses of several users of Agent Orange were being kept. The sight of those corpses . . . men and women with their eyes bulging like oranges growing out of their faces and their brains popped out of their skulls like orange popcorn—

No. I'm going to find an antidote, cure, fix, whatever you want to call it, for this, if it kills me.

Prophetic words maybe, but Dr. Annabelle Cole had no idea of that now.

Annabelle crossed the extensive laboratory, an academic scowl on her face as she considered the importance of the work she was involved in here.

And where is Doyle? Lunch break was over fifteen minutes ago.

Her assistant Doyle Sanders was a constant source of irritation to her. Though undoubtedly brilliant, to her well-educated mind the young man lacked something important.

Before taking up her position here at F-Bio, Annabelle had lectured at West Virginia University. Doyle reminded her of some of her students back then, all of them unquestionably brilliant but equally lacking that same 'something' that would make them top-notch researchers.

And what is that something? she asked herself as she reached the dissection slab where a rabbit lay pinned spreadeagled and with its bright orange brain revealed because its skull had been removed.

Annabelle replied to her own question: Something they were missing was simply the desire to acquire knowledge for its own sake— the desire to understand a thing, not because it would *benefit or hurt humanity, nature, or the environment, but simply because you desire to know!*

She herself wasn't lacking in such amoral curiosity. Consider this current situation. Yes, the cops wanted her expert opinion on why

Agent Orange was so addictive—and if possible, also wanted a drug that could counter or reverse the effects of the narcotic (both, if possible). But, beyond that, Annabelle desired to know—she felt a thrill at the quest for this secret knowledge—she desired—purely for its own sake—to tread the same dark corridors the late Max Carillo had while inventing his amped-up version of crack cocaine.

Annabelle stared down at the pinned rabbit. Even with its skullcap peeled away and its brain exposed, it wasn't dead by a long shot. The piebald animal was still gnashing its teeth at her, and, but for the fact that its neck was restrained by a metal hoop pinned down on the wooden dissecting block, and its hips similarly constrained, Annabelle knew the damned thing would have ripped its pinned limbs right off their metal nails and leaped up to sink its teeth in her throat.

Once again, she was unable to determine if the motivation in its little exposed orange brain was anger or hunger.

But back to Annabelle's earlier train of thought. Though undeniably brilliant, her young colleague and assistant Doyle Sanders clearly lacked that 'science for science's sake' mentality.

She once more glanced down at the rabbit.

Crazy, just crazy, she thought as it futilely snapped its jaws at her, then she glanced down at her wristwatch. *And where the hell is Doyle?*

And right then, Doyle Sanders walked in through the lab's farther door.

Annabelle turned around and frowned at him. "Where the hell were you?"

Doyle grinned his regular grin. "Sorry, boss, but poop is a respecter of no man."

Annabelle decided to let it go. Doyle Sanders was a difficult person to stay mad at.

CHAPTER 2

"Did I miss anything?" Doyle asked as he hurried over to his superior's side.

"Not really." Annabelle gestured down at the pinned rabbit. "I'm just getting ready to work on Mr. Bunny here."

Doyle concealed a sigh of relief. Though his supervisor, Dr. Cole, was a very fair woman, Doyle felt he was walking the thin line of taking liberty for a license. This was far from his first or even fifth late lunch break.

And the reason? No, Doyle hadn't needed to use the toilet like he'd told his supervisor. He'd actually been arguing with his girlfriend Anita on the phone.

"You never have time for me nowadays," Anita had been complaining. Doyle agreed somewhat reasonably because she was between jobs at the moment and, as such, had a lot of free time on her hands.

"Listen," he finally told her after a desperate glance at the time on his cellphone. Today's Friday, we're already at the weekend. You have me all to yourself for the next two days."

"I doubt that. Your boss will most likely just monopolize you again. Like she did last weekend."

"She won't. Her daughter's coming up from uni this weekend. She always takes time off to spend time with her. They'll likely go camping or something."

"We should go camping too."

"We will."

"That's Good. It's irritating that you spend more time with that old woman than you do with me."

"Hey, hey, Dr. Cole isn't old, and maybe you should get a job."

"I told you, I'm not waitressing again. And, baby, you're supposed to be helping me get a job with Tony. I've told you to ask him. The guy is bound to have something for me."

"I already *did* ask him. And I told you—he's working on something. Just give him a little time. In the meantime, you gotta have patience. Unless you wanna work as a stripper at that club of his."

Anita had sighed over the phone. "Meaning, I gotta find a way to kill my boredom. Maybe I'll come by the lab to see you."

"Oh no. Dr. Cole won't like it."

"See? There she comes between us again."

"Okay, I gotta run," Doyle had told Anita after another look at his cellphone. He'd abruptly ended the call and then headed for the lab.

Now, he stared down at the rabbit with the exposed brain. Dammit. Doyle had never seen a chemical substance that altered the color of human flesh like that. And the rabbit's eyes too—looking like someone had amped up the amber in traffic lights.

Max Carillo was a madman genius for sure, Doyle thought. *And we reap the positives and negatives of his actions. The doc sees only the negatives. Me, I can see some positives as well.*

In the meantime, Dr. Cole had filled a hypodermic syringe with liquified Agent Orange and was preparing to inject it into their rabbit test subject, the aim of this experiment to view at first hand the effect of controlled doses of Agent Orange on the animal brain.

"Hey, doc, don't you think that's a little too much?" Doyle asked a little uneasily.

Dr. Cole paused with the syringe touching the rabbit's neck and shook her head. "Not at all. This is the same dosage of Agent Orange that we've been administering all along. Remember why we agreed on this amount, Doyle; with the idea being that we needed an amount—nothing too small, mind you—an amount that would produce visible and thus easily registrable changes in the subject's physiology and anatomy, with the idea being that such noticeable changes would enable us to easily track the progress of the animal's addiction."

Her hand quivered slightly, and she accidentally jabbed the rabbit in the neck, producing a slight trickle of blood, even though she'd not yet injected it with the chemical in the hypo. "And, Doyle, so far it's worked. "We now know the exact dosage that causes a rabbit's eyes to assume this horrible orange color and we even have an idea as to why it does so—"

"But doc,"

She raised the hypo and wagged it in his face. "Please let me finish, kid. I was about to say that calculations using this knowledge already enable us to work out how much Agent Orange will produce similar reactions in humans." She smiled. "Yes, I know—police forensics already knows that, and I admit their results parallel our findings. But remember, we're conducting research here."

Doyle didn't comment. Up to a point, he agreed with his boss. But there was something about the way this current rabbit looked (lots of others had already made the short trip to rabbit hell via the laboratory incinerator) that had him worried. Not it's still aggravated state, which oddly seemed to have relaxed a little bit now that its little junkie brain had realized its human captors were about to shoot it up again, but something else.

Staring at the rabbit, with its swollen eyes like crazy orange grapes, was making Doyle feel mega-uneasy,

"Anyway," Dr. Cole went on. "What I'm getting at here is that now we've also established the threshold for irreversible brain transformation, and we understand that the act of synthesizing an effect counter for Agent Orange will involve a substance that acts on—"

"Yes, but can we halve the dose?" Doyle asked. "This little fellow here looks like he's taken all the Agent Orange his little brain can cope with."

Dr. Cole shook her head. "Nope, and don't insist. We'll complete this particular experiment at the dosage level we set at the beginning."

Understanding that he'd lost the argument, Doyle Sanders nodded. He watched grimly while his boss injected the captive rabbit in the neck with the full syringe of orange narcotic. After doing so, Dr. Cole dropped the hypo and she and Doyle both waited and watched. The rabbit for its part, now lay limp, with its body twitching as if thrilling in ecstasy.

"See, your worries were quite unfounded," Dr. Cole said. "Our little subject here is simply—"

Then she shut up as the rabbit's head split completely in two and its brains popped out of its little face. It was an incredible sight to behold, as this time the animal's brains had also swollen to more than the size of its body.

"Yeah, I guess we did give it too much Agent Orange," Dr. Cole agreed with a sigh. "But at least now we know the exact dosage that will kill a rabbit and, by extrapolation, a human being." She gave Doyle a calculating look. "And now, kid, do me the honor of packing the remains up for the incinerator."

Doyle got to work with bagging the dead rabbit and dumping it into the lab's 'biological waste' bin.

CHAPTER 3

After bagging and safely disposing of the dead rabbit, the next order of lab business was to feed the other animals.

This too was a job that fell to Doyle. Dr. Annabelle Cole found feeding time too icky with these test animals. She preferred nice white non-violent lab mice, which didn't look like they hated you.

"Hey, Doyle feed the critters, will you?" she said nicely.

"Sure, boss," Doyle called back and got to work on it.

Feeding time consisted of two separate jobs. First of all, Doyle fed the rodents raw meat, mostly steaks. Initially, he'd tried the rats and rabbits out with grains and nuts and carrots—recommended stuff like that, but all had ignored the vegetarian fare. So, it had been raw meat from then on.

Once, on Dr. Cole's instructions, Doyle had fed the caged rodents one of their dead fellows. The others had eaten it all up, orange brain included. The cannibalized rodent's gnawed bones still decorated their cages, since neither scientist had worked out how to safely remove them from in there.

Now, Doyle dropped a fat slab of bloody meat into the feeding trough at the front of each 'cell,' and then watched the animals eat.

In the meantime, Dr. Cole was logging the latest test results. Occasionally, she whispered to herself.

Doyle watched her for a while, then pulled out a candy bar from the pocket of his lab coat and bit into it. When he was through with the bar, he dropped the wrapper on the long wooden shelf on which the cages stood and walked over to attend to the second part of feeding the animals.

"Doyle, you forgot the candy wrapper again," Dr. Cole reminded him while he tapped in the code to the laboratory vault.

"Yeah, yeah, doc, I'll deal with it later," Doyle said dutifully, while pulling open the vault door.

The vault stood in the corner opposite the laboratory door. Most of its contents were precious specimens, rare chemicals, and research papers. But on its lowest shelf sat a fat bag of Agent Orange.

The Agent Orange in the vault had been synthesized here in the F-Bio lab. This had been necessary because the original amount of Agent Orange available had been too little for the needed research. However, the police had recovered the formula for Agent Orange amongst Max Carillo's research papers, and for a biochemical facility, where complicated chemicals were regularly synthesized, Agent Orange had proved to be very easy to make.

Manufacturing Agent Orange was Doyle's job, too. Once he'd cooked a sufficient amount of the narcotic, he shut it away in the vault. Seeing as their research here was ongoing, Doyle found himself cooking up Agent Orange on a weekly basis.

Now, Doyle got out ten chunks of the orange marshmallow-like substance from the package and carried it over towards the animals.

The caged animals could smell the Agent Orange and it had an electric effect on them. Some of them tensed up, while others flung themselves against the railing of their cages. One rabbit somehow forced its head between the bars of its cage and began spitting randomly in every direction. It was both scary and pathetic to witness.

Okay, Doyle didn't enjoy this part of feeding time either, and he understood why Dr. Cole left him to do it. It wasn't just seniority at play; there was a damning expression of craziness here, something of which the doctor clearly wanted no part.

"Okay, here you go, furry guys and girls," Doyle said, while he dropped the chunks of Agent Orange into the feeding troughs. Then he stepped back and watched the animals eat. Watching them eat made him feel hungry, so he dipped in his lab coat pocket again and fished around inside a bag of shelled peanuts he had in there. He ate messily, not watching where he was dropping the peanut shells; a good number of which ended up on the floor of the laboratory, rather than inside the pocket they'd been intended for. Actually, Doyle wasn't even conscious that he was making a mess.

Doyle was popping unshelled nuts into his mouth, staring almost in a trance at the orange-eyed animals which now seemed in a similar state of trance as they consumed the drug he'd just bestowed on them. Several of the rabbits seemed to enter a Zen state when this happened. They just stood where they were, rigid as statues, with their bright orange eyes bulging and the veins in their heads visibly pulsating beneath their fur.

It was both wonderful and scary to witness.

Then Doyle felt Dr. Cole tap him on the shoulder.

Startled, and with a mouth full of peanuts, he spun around from staring at the animals to stare at her instead.

"How is it, that as brainy as you are, you can't get it into your head that you need to be tidier?" she asked him, gesturing down at the mess of peanut shells on the floor. "This is a bioresearch laboratory, for chrissakes! You know as well as I do that we can't risk sample contamination."

Doyle sighed. This wasn't the first time she'd pointed out this simple and obvious fact to him. "I'll clean it up," he said, then, by way of explanation, gestured at the caged animals. "I just get entranced staring at them."

She gave him a cold and uncharacteristic look. "It's not just that, Doyle," she said, pointing down between the end of one of the tables that ran along the wall and a short laboratory cabinet, where—horror of horrors—a cockroach, of all nasty things, was making its unconcerned way along the angle between the wall and the floor. "I've got the feeling that that's your fault too."

"Ah, boss, that's unfair," Doyle quickly countered in his defense, before she turned on the accusation taps full blast. He'd been in the process of fishing a peanut out of the package—the unshelled had now gotten mixed up with the shelled, and he was having trouble separating them—but he decided to leave off eating them for now. Doc had that look on her face that spoke of her still being disappointed by the failure of their most recent experiment.

Well, I did warn her we were giving Drugs Bunny too much medication.

"Unfair?" Dr. Cole said, in some irritation. "Doyle, you're a brilliant young man—you may even be a genius—but you're something of a slob." After gesturing over at where the wrapper of his recently eaten Mars Bar dangled on the edge of the cage shelf, seemingly pondering whether or not to fall to the floor, she looked pointedly at him. "Alright, tell me; you're supposed to be clean-shaven. When last did you shave?"

Doyle unconsciously ran a finger over his chin. She was right; his chin itched. He hadn't shaved in days, and what had originally been five o'clock stubble would soon grow into a beard. "Aw, boss, gimme a break. You know how busy we always are here."

She nodded. "I keep giving you breaks, kid." Then she sighed. "Yes, I do. But how are we supposed to carry out reliable research with cockroaches in the lab?"

Then a thought seemed to cross her mind, because she added, while pointing to the gap by the specimen cabinet, where another roach had now joined the previous one: "You know, this is the third time I've noticed roaches in this lab, and they're always over there. I wonder what's responsible. There has to be something back there that's attracting them."

"Hey, hey, boss, take it easy," advised Doyle, when she stepped towards the cabinet, causing the roaches to all vanish back beneath the table, where, because the table had lots of drawers built into it, they were invisible. Doyle, who knew exactly what the roaches were finding so irresistible behind the lab table, also quickly stepped into her path to block her off.

"Don't bother," he said. "I think I spilled something down there. Anyway, I'll try to fumigate the lab over the weekend." He frowned and jabbed a thumb over at the orange-eyed animals, which, now that they'd had their daily fix of Agent Orange, seemed both calmer and more irritated. "I'll have to move our furry friends out of here while it's done . . . but I'll discuss it with Riley tomorrow. At the very least, we'll set up a few roach motels around the place to deal with the bugs. Like the ad says, they'll check in, but won't check out again."

Dr. Cole nodded and made no attempt to walk past him. She clearly hadn't really wanted a ringside view of the cockroaches.

"Okay, you do that," she quickly agreed. "But please, try to be neater—less messy from now on. Just imagine what would happen if those roaches get into something problematic—like Agent Orange, for instance."

Doyle had to laugh at that. "Aw, c'mon, doc; now you're imagining things. There's absolutely no chance of cockroaches getting into the vault where Agent Orange is stored." He gestured over at the caged rodents. "And you know those little guys sure as hell won't share their share of the drug with the roaches. They'll rather eat the roaches instead."

The 'little guys' in question glared nastily at Doyle and the doctor like they understood what the former was saying.

Dr. Cole nodded. "Yeah, I guess you're right."

"Sure I am, doc," Doyle said airily and then hurried off to get a broom and dustpan to sweep up the mess he'd made.

CHAPTER 4

The reason why there were now cockroaches in F-Bio's previously pristine Lab 7 was because, about a fortnight ago, Doyle had accidentally lost part of a hamburger down between the back of the table and the wall.

How this happened requires a little explanation. It was simple really. Doyle had just been finishing up work for the day, when his girlfriend Anita had called to pick him up. Doyle was absentminded at the best of times, constantly forgetting where he'd dropped things. Anita had brought along a hamburger for Doyle.

And then, while Doyle had been eating his hamburger, Anita had suddenly gotten it into her mind to have sex in the laboratory. It was simply a whim, and Doyle had obliged her.

But to have sex required Doyle putting down his hamburger somewhere, and he'd chosen the top of the table that almost abutted on the specimen cabinet. This turned out to be a less than foresightful choice when he and Anita realized that the table was exactly the right height for him to penetrate her. It was uncanny, really, how perfectly her pussy lined up with Doyle's dick when he got her seated on the edge of the table. But before any comfortable penetration could be achieved, the few objects on the table—scientific (lab stuff), fashionable (Anita's handbag), and edible (the hamburger in question), needed to be cleared out of the way.

Because they'd both been so horny at the time, this had all been accomplished in a summary fashion (by the left-right swipe of hands) with no real attention being paid to what had ended up where. The sole reason why Anita's handbag hadn't gone behind the table with the two-thirds consumed hamburger and three test tubes was because it was too big to fit down there.

Anyway, they'd had nice sex and nice orgasms. Afterwards Doyle had remembered his burger, and a brief search had revealed it was stuck behind the table, in an awkward position that the closeness of the table to the wall (along with the furniture's set of built-in drawers) made it impossible to access. True, the burger could have been dislodged from its location with a broom handle, but in true afterglow fashion, by then Doyle felt winded from the sex, and so balked at making the effort.

So, he and Anita had left the burger where it was and gone out clubbing.

This had occurred on a Friday night and by Monday morning, the hamburger had been forgotten as completely as Friday night's orgasm.

The fact that this was a biochemistry lab, and as such a location that was filled with pungent chemical odors on a daily basis, only helped Doyle's loss of memory of the discarded burger.

And then, one night a lab window was left open, and several cockroaches found their way into the laboratory, found the now stale and moldy hamburger behind the table, and decided that F-Bio's Lab 7 wasn't that bad a place to nest in for a while.

CHAPTER 5

Park ranger Gary Bentley was relaxing after a hard day's work.

It had been a normal enough day. Walking the park trails, checking that the animals weren't in distress, watching for fire hazards and making certain campers adhered to fire safety and littering regulations.

But now, all Gary wanted was to kick up his soles, watch a game on TV and relax, while he sat beside his wife Charlotte. Of course, being with Charlotte meant a war for control of the remote control. As always, Charlotte wanted to watch a romantic comedy. Gary knew he'd give in finally and let her have the remote like he always did, but at first he doggedly refused to let her change the channel from the news.

"Isn't it great how there's nothing about that creepy Agent Orange on the TV nowadays," Charlotte said after they'd dueled over the remote for a while, a duel now stalemated because Gary, who already had a loving arm around Charlotte's shoulder, had now used this positional advantage to hold her arm in place. She, however, felt nicely snug like this, and so let him have his way.

Gary thought on that for a moment, then laughed. "Yeah, I know what you mean. "It's like the drug's gone out of fashion since that crackhead bigfoot caper."

"Oh, honey, stop it," Charlotte giggled. "Bigfoot is a myth. That was just a bear you guys ran into up on the mountain."

"That weren't no bear," Gary said. "You oughta have seen it, girl."

Charlotte shrugged. "Well, I didn't. And no one else did either. At least no one who survived"

"The psychic lady, Amelia Blackwood did. She saw it too."

"Gimme a break, darling. A psychic woman seeing bigfoot. Even if I was gonna take you seriously before, that single reference just nixed it. Believing in psychics is worse than believing in the Easter Bunny."

Gary laughed, but let it go. Charlotte had never believed he'd actually encountered bigfoot and only escaped alive by the skin of his teeth. And yet who could blame her? Some days, Gary didn't believe it himself.

He directed his thoughts back to her initial point; that of recent there had been less news about Agent Orange.

"You're right," he told his wife with a smile. "Of recent, no people—and more importantly—no *animals*, honey, are getting doped up on that addictive orange candy."

She smiled back. "You think the worst is over, now that Max Carillo is dead?"

Gary nodded back at her. "Yep, I sure do, honey. At least, I hope so." His expression turned pensive, his brow furrowed up in thought, and for the few seconds while he said the next few words, he looked years older: "Of course, in cases like this, it's impossible to be a hundred percent sure the scourge is over. But at the moment the cops have a handle on things, so that's a positive."

"They've stopped its manufacture then?"

Gary shook his head. "Not yet, hon. My friends on the force say they've gotten most of the local dealers in custody. But, they're still having trouble locating the source of the drug."

Charlotte Bentley gave her husband a surprised look. "I thought that guy Max was the only one cooking Agent Orange?"

"I used to think so too," Gary said. "But law enforcement aren't sure. There's at least one major supplier still operating in this area. Cops ain't got no leads on him yet tho'."

Realizing that continuing this discussion might ruin what had so far been a pleasant evening for them both, Gary Bentley handed Charlotte the remote control and gestured at the TV. "Okay, honey, you win," he said with a laugh. "Pick whatever you want to watch. But best make it something good, or else you'll watch it alone."

Charlotte eventually found something they both liked: binge-watching the Kiefer Sutherland *24* series.

They settled down to watch it.

But although Gary Bentley really enjoyed the movie, he couldn't shake a cold feeling at the back of his mind. At a point in time, it seemed to him as if the mere mention of the drug Agent Orange by he and his wife was willing its terrifying evil back into existence.

Oh no, I gotta stop thinking like this, he told himself. *Agent Orange is simply a bad memory that won't go away.*

Then, Gary wondered why he'd thought that. What he really thought was that the bad memories the drug brought to his mind would fade with time.

Of course, they will. It's just a matter of time till the damn drug itself is out of circulation.

Somehow, however, Gary was unable to convince himself that this really would be the case. The more cynical side of his mind seemed to insist that it was merely a matter of time before another monumental Agent Orange fuckup happened. And, worryingly, seeing as it had been a full month since the last disaster, this town and its woods were about overdue for the next installment.

CHAPTER 6

That Friday night at the Futures Bioresearch facility, Doyle Sanders sat down to cook up some Agent Orange.

The time now was a quarter past ten. Except for the small nook where Doyle sat with his equipment, the lab lighting was dimmed.

Occasionally as Doyle worked, mixing baking soda with cocaine and those other more esoteric compounds that Max Curillo's formula specified and cooking the results to the dead man's specifications, he stared over at the animal cages.

The animals were restive; they smelled the source of their addiction being created, and the smell was like God in their brains. They hissed and spat, but mostly sat silent, worshippers awed and terrified by the incomprehensible greatness they sensed a short distance from their constrained existence.

"I'll give you all a little in a little bit," Doyle told them cheerily while overseeing his chemical work.

***

If the West Virginian police were looking for the new source of Agent Orange, they needed to look no further than Doyle Sanders, a young man who clearly wasn't even on their suspect list.

Ever since Max Curillo's death, Doyle had taken over Agent Orange production in the state and was turning a steady and growing profit.

Doyle found it ironic that the cops were themselves providing part of the cocaine that he was converting to the dreaded Agent Orange. But the police had an excess of drug dealer coke on their shelves, evidence left over from trials, and how better to utilize that leftover cocaine than by dedicating it to scientific research designed to counter drug usage.

So, the cops had unwittingly provided Doyle with the initial cocaine he'd converted to Agent Orange. He'd banked the profits from that and replaced the cocaine in the lab vault, and no one was the wiser.

And now I'm the chief supplier in the state of WV, he thought. Quite an achievement for a guy like me.

In considering what was seemingly lacking in Doyle's scientific makeup, Dr. Annabelle Cole had missed out on one characteristic: Doyle was only interested in science for profit. That was the whole reason he'd applied to work at F-Bio in the first place; he was interested in participating in a scientific breakthrough that would make him rich.

And if Agent Orange doesn't exactly cure cancer, it's definitely a fast track to wealth for me; he thought as he set aside a fresh batch of orange chemical bliss to cool. *It works for me anyhow.* Doyle laughed. *A few months ago, a girl like Anita wouldn't even give me the time of day, and now she's already suggesting a trip to visit my mother.*

Doyle laughed and looked over at the caged animals. They amused him with their expressions of stoned reverence to the chemical glory he was creating. He felt nothing for them other than this amusement, just as he felt nothing—no twinges of conscience about the people whose lives the drug he sold was guaranteed to ruin. Doyle viewed them like they were animals.

Their fucking faults, not mine. I didn't give them addictive personalities. And no one's forcing them to smoke this shit. I'm just a simple businessman who's matching supply to demand. And to my advantage, demand is high and growing exponentially, despite the best efforts of the boys in blue to curb it.

Doyle smiled coldly as he prepared a fresh mix. Then he scowled as a fat black cockroach walked along the tabletop towards him. The roach, possibly attracted by the remains of Doyle's spaghetti takeout which lay on the tabletop, walked closer, until Doyle tilted over a Bunsen burner and fried it in the gas flame. The burner left a dark patch on the work surface. The roach's charred remains made an even darker patch.

Remembering that he was supposed to talk to the janitor Riley about those roach motel traps tomorrow, Doyle got back to work. Then after working for a while, Doyle figured there was no point telling the janitor about the roaches.

It ain't like the lab's infested with them; it's just this spot behind this single table, and I know exactly why there's bugs there anyway. There's no reason to move all of the test animals and fumigate the lab just for that reason. I'll just buy some roach traps myself and set them up in here.

Then his phone buzzed. He smiled when he saw it was Anita.

"Hey, baby," she said when he picked up. "Are you missing me?"

Doyle laughed. Behind Anita, he could hear the party a friend of theirs was giving. Loud music and people dancing. The sounds made him feel really good.

Yeah, this nerd is definitely coming up in the world, he thought.

"I *am* missing you," he replied to his girlfriend. "What time are you coming by to pick me up?"

"That's actually why I'm calling. Are you ready yet so I can drive over?"

Doyle glanced at the clock on the wall to his left and did a quick mental calculation. "I'll be finished here in thirty minutes."

"Okay, I'll leave in fifteen."

She hung up, and Doyle smiled, picturing her pretty face, short black hair, and heart-shaped pout.

The car was actually his, but Anita insisted on driving it, so he'd let her have it. So long as she didn't wrap the Nissan around a tree or lamppost Doyle didn't mind fueling it.

Of course, she could be using the car to pick up some other guy while I'm working here and sucking his dick in my backseat.

But Doyle didn't think that was the case. Anita seemed to be way too into him for that kind of sleazy behavior.

***

The noise of a car made Doyle wonder if Anita had left Jasmine's party early. He peeked out through the laboratory window and saw distant headlights heading up towards the research facility. But suddenly, the headlights swerved to the right and vanished from sight—not Anita, then.

With the Agent Orange mix bubbling over a Bunsen burner, Doyle stared out into the night for a while longer. He tried to see past the perimeter fence, but the lights that illuminated the wire barricade made this difficult. It was just grass out there anyway, and then trees and mountains.

The facility's isolation made sense. Out here on the edge of town, it was easier to minimize the damage from spillages of dangerous chemicals, chemical fires, or even explosions. Of course, one had to balance that knowledge with the realization that it would also take much longer for help to reach them in case of such a crisis. But F-Bio paid its staff well, and no one was complaining.

Doyle turned his focus back to the job at hand, cooking up his Agent Orange. Tonight, he was making a larger amount of the substance than usual. Tony, a friend/customer of his who owned a strip joint over on Broadway, had requested some product. While Doyle didn't actually relish the thought of crack-addicted strippers, business was business, and a dollar was a dollar. So, he cooked up the stuff as requested and bagged it.

While Doyle worked, he ran his mind over the chemical properties of Agent Orange. One of the most incredible things about this particular crack variant (and what, to his mind, really proved Max Curillo"s genius) was the fact that, unlike regular crack, this Agent Orange shit was water-soluble. So, in addition to smoking it, you could snort it like the regular white stuff, eat it, drink it, inject it; in short, you could imbibe the stuff any which way you wanted.

Though the intensity of the resulting high did indeed vary depending on the route by which the orange narcotic entered the user's body, the desired end result—getting high—would still be achieved to some degree.

Doyle's thoughts were interrupted by the sight of another cockroach; down on the floor this time. The roach was investigating one of those peanuts Doyle had dropped earlier in the day and later missed sweeping up with the others.

Doyle watched the brown oblong-shaped bug for a while, finally losing interest in it at about the same time as it lost interest in the peanut. The roach vanished back beneath the table.

Doyle made a mental note that he really needed to get those roach motel traps set up in the lab, or at very least buy a king-sized can of insecticide.

This batch of Agent Orange he was cooking was the last lot. It was now ready. He retrieved the drug chunks, dried them up, and bagged it with the rest, and then weighed the lot. Slightly over a pound's worth, which was what Tony had ordered.

So, we'll just head over to the strip club once Anita shows up and hand it to him. Then she and I can go party and relax. She owes me a blowjob at least.

Outside, he noticed the headlights of another approaching car, this one continuing up the road towards the research facility. Meaning Anita was here and he'd better get the lab cleaned up and head out to the parking lot to meet her.

As his last order of business before he left tonight, Doyle decided to keep his joking promise to the caged animals. First of all, he poked around in his freshly cooked stash for little chunks to feed to them. But then he changed his mind. The packaged weighed a pound, which was what Tony had requested. If he took out of it, he'd be reducing the weight, and he didn't want to have to tap into his emergency stash to make up the difference.

Besides it was Friday night; time to party a bit with his girlfriend.

So instead, he decided to feed the animals from the Agent Orange stored in the vault. That was what it was there for.

Doyle walked over to the vault, got out some Agent Orange chunks and walked over to the waiting animals in their cages. He loved the way the little furry addicts stared at him as he approached them, like they'd shifted their initial reverence of the smell in the lab to reverence of his physical presence.

They're staring at me like I'm God.

'God' fed his caged 'worshippers.'

After sealing up the package of innocent-looking orange 'marshmallows' that he'd just manufactured, Doyle cleaned up the worksurface as quickly as he could. While brushing the charred cockroach down onto the floor, he scowled at the burnt patch killing it had left on the tabletop. *The boss is gonna chew me out for that mistake. I'd better think up a really good excuse.* But the bug had annoyed him, so . . .

Doyle finally got everything cleaned up and put away, but not before he'd killed another roach—this time less extravagantly, as he just stomped the thing into mush.

He removed his lab coat, and washed his hands, then bent over to pick up the package of Agent Orange and leave the lab.

"Doyle, what are you doing here this late?"

Doyle froze. That wasn't Anita's voice. It was Dr. Cole's. *Shit! I mistook her car for mine!* A cold dagger of panic stabbed him in the back of his neck and began slicing down his spine.

If she sees this package of drugs, I'm going to jail for sure.

"Doyle, I'm talking to you."

From the sound of her voice, Doyle could tell that Dr. Annabelle Cole was still a few yards behind him. Thinking desperately, he did the only thing that came to mind. He leaned forward and pushed the bag of Agent Orange out of sight between the table and the wall. Dr. Cole seemed to be standing out of view of his hands, and he hoped the sound of the package striking the wall and slipping out of view wouldn't arouse her suspicions that anything was amiss.

"Doyle, are you alright?"

Now, Dr. Cole was standing directly behind him. He felt her fingers tentatively touch his shoulder.

"Doyle?" she said again.

Putting on the best act he could, Doyle spun around and stared at her with a startled look on his face.

"Doc? Damn, you scared the shit out of me!"

She took a step back, and nodded. "Sorry 'bout that. But what are you doing here at this hour? The security guys said you came back about an hour ago and hadn't left yet."

Doyle nodded. "Yeah, yeah. I forgot a present I bought for Anita, and came back to the lab to look for it."

While saying this he examined her aging face for signs that she'd noticed him concealing the Agent Orange. But she only sniffed the air. "Something smells burnt in here."

Doyle felt slightly relieved by her statement, and again wondered how to explain the burnt patch on the workbench. But he didn't need to, because the next thing Dr. Cole asked him was: "So, did you find it?"

"Huh? What?" Doyle had forgotten his own lie, but he quickly recovered. "Oh, no. It's not in here. I've spent close to an hour searching everywhere, including in the toilets."

Annabelle Cole now looked perplexed. "The toilets? Why would you take your girlfriend's present in there?"

Doyle laughed. "Not intentionally. It's a necklace and pendant. Very cute, but also easy to lose."

Dr. Cole laughed too. "Oh, I understand." After saying this, she seemed to lose interest in the subject altogether. She turned away from Doyle, and walked over towards the caged animals. "Oh, I see you've fed our little junkies again."

He nodded. "They kept staring at me . . . wouldn't quit. It's unnerving to see. I figured if they had a snack, they'd forget about me. I don't think it worked though."

Doyle was trying to work out how to retrieve the package of Agent Orange from where he'd hidden it without the doctor noticing. If only she'd leave the lab for a few minutes, maybe to visit the restroom. But no, Dr. Cole had seated herself at her desk and was turning on her laptop. Doyle cursed. *If only I'd stashed the drugs in my laptop bag. But they were still hot.*

And as he watched his supervisor, Doyle Sanders suddenly realized he'd made a huge mistake in where he'd chosen to conceal his freshly-cooked narcotic: he'd shoved the package down the same space where he'd lost his burger a fortnight ago, that narrow gap between table and wall, and just like the burger, the package of Agent Orange hadn't fallen all the way down to the floor.

Shit, there's no way I'm gonna dislodge it from there without using a broomstick. Meaning there's no way I can get the drugs tonight, with the doc here in the lab.

Outside of the lab, another set of headlights were approaching the F-Bio block of buildings. Anita was finally arriving. Time to leave. He wouldn't be able to hang around once she was here.

Trying not to show how frustrated her presence here was making him, Doyle asked Dr. Cole. "So, what brings you here tonight, boss?"

She looked up from reading figures on her laptop. "I just realized I've some work I need to get through tonight, if I'm gonna spend the weekend with my daughter."

"Boss, the lab will still be here on Monday. Go home and get some rest."

She sighed. "Unlike you, kid, my mind won't let me forget my work responsibilities. If I don't handle this work stuff tonight, thoughts of it are gonna plague me all weekend and ruin my quality time with Jenny."

Doyle nodded and conceded defeat. *I'll have to supply Tony from my emergency supply over at the cabin. But then, that's what the emergency supply was designed for, for cases like this, when shit goes wrong.*

"Okay, boss, I'll be on my way," he told Dr. Cole, then picked up his laptop bag and turned to leave.

"Hey, Doyle, you're forgetting something."

He turned back towards her. What had he forgotten? He had a moment's panic that the bag of Agent Orange had slid down to the floor of its own accord and she'd noticed it. But from where he stood across the room, nothing was visible beneath the bottom of the table, which, due to its built-in drawers, almost reached to the floor itself, which was the very reason stuff that fell and got stuck behind it proved so hard to retrieve.

Dr. Cole pointed towards the tabletop, where the remains of Doyle's last meal sat amidst the glittering beakers, test tubes, and Bunsen burners. "Doyle, how many times do I need to remind you to clean up after yourself? Slovenliness like this seems almost a habit with you."

Doyle managed to grin, and then he hurried back over to the table to pack up the fast-food bag.

He scowled on noticing that two fat cockroaches were already investigating the chicken bones and other scraps in the bag. The damned things were getting bolder!

With a look of disgust on his face, Doyle folded up the bag with the roaches still inside it, and then carried it over to a trash can.

"Okay, I'm leaving for good now," he told Dr. Cole with a wave in her direction.

She waved back. "Okay, man, have a good weekend. Give my regards to Anita."

Doyle left the lab, pissed off at himself for losing Tony's Agent Orange behind the table. He was also disgusted at how the roaches had been playing around in his food. He hoped they'd not gotten into the food while he'd still been eating it.

Then he tried to put all of that out of his mind; he might as well go enjoy the evening with Anita.

CHAPTER 7

In the F-Bio parking lot, Doyle found Anita balanced against the hood of the car, waiting for him.

Anita __ was tall, slim and very pretty. She was the sister of a friend of Doyle's and he'd admired her from afar when he didn't have the money to show her a good time. Back then she'd made it clear that, yeah, he might be cute and all that, but his good-looks wouldn't pay her bills. Not that she was really able to pay her own bills either— Doyle thought it was foolhardy, trying to be high-maintenance on a waitressing job. Still, she'd acted as if she had standards to meet, and he didn't meet them.

But now that he had all this drug money? Anita didn't give a shit about where his income came from, and that made sense to Doyle: gangster's girlfriends and wives never went to jail, so if he took a fall, she'd be in the clear. All she'd have to do was turn evidence for the prosecution and claim he was manipulating her. And then, once he was behind bars, she'd start sucking the next dishonest dick in line.

That's just how the game is played, Doyle thought with a cold smile. *So, as far as I'm concerned, I'd better not get caught.*

***

"Hey, baby," she said, when he reached her and then she kissed him.

"Let's roll," Doyle said when they separated.

They got into the car, and Anita grinned over at him. "So, where to? Are you hungry, or do we head straight back to Jasmine's party?"

Doyle shook his head. "First of all I've got to call Tony."

Anita gestured at Doyle's laptop bag. "You got his stuff ready, right?"

Doyle decided he loved how amoral his new girlfriend was. Anita being in on his drug dealing took a lot of pressure off of his mind.

"Nope," he said. "I don't got Tony's drugs ready."

Her surprise was exactly what he'd anticipated. "Why not, baby? That is why you came back here by yourself."

Doyle told her what had happened.

She listened and then shrugged: "So, do you want us to come back for it later?"

Doyle made a vague gesture towards the nearby mountains. "No need. I'll just dip into the emergency stash out at the cabin."

Anita nodded. Do you want us to drive out there now?"

"It's too late. Just let me call Tony."

She waited while he dialed. After a few rings, Tony Lopez answered. It sounded like Tony was outside of his office at the strip club. Doyle could hear music in the background and scattered voices.

"Hey, bro, what's happening?" asked Tony. "As promised, the cash is ready. You got my shit ready?"

"Yes and no."

"What the fuck does that mean?"

Doyle explained about the slight mishap in the laboratory. "Hey, but there's no problem. I've got a backup stash stored up near the campground."

"I dunno, Doyle. Problem is, the drugs ain't for me. You know I don't use that wacky orange shit. I was there when that shit cracked a friend's face wide open like a walnut, and his brains spilled out all orange in color. That was enough for me. Weed and blow are enough for me."

"Yeah, I'd wondered about that," Doyle said, putting the phone on speaker so Anita could follow their conversation. "You don't strike me as an orangehead yourself, and the last thing you can possibly want is a joint full of crack-addicted strippers."

Tony laughed. "You're right about that last. I had to let two girls go last week, 'cos they were using meth."

"So, who's the Agent Orange for then?"

"I have an Ex-army buddy named Bobby. I don't know how he got into Agent Orange, but he and his girl are hardcore users. When I told them I knew a guy who could hook them up, they looked at me like I was Jesus Christ."

"They're gonna have to wait, man," Doyle said. "It's too late tonight for me to head in the woods. I don't wanna run into any bears. But tomorrow morning's cool."

"Hey, make that tomorrow afternoon," Anita said. "Tonight's party night. I'm gonna need a long lay-in tomorrow morning."

"Hey, who's that there with you?" Tony asked with a worried note in his voice.

"My super-hot girlfriend."

"Anita is listening to us?"

"Don't worry about it, bro. She's cool. The lady works with me."

"If you say so, man." There was a pause, and then Tony added: "Well, I guess it'll have to be tomorrow afternoon, then. I'll let the guys know what's happened. Hey, Doyle?"

"Yeah?"

"You're sure we ain't gonna have any more delays? These two friends of mind are quite manic. I don't wanna get on their bad side if you disappoint me again."

"Dude, don't worry about it. The drugs exist. It's my emergency stash for times such as this."

"Okay, bro," Tony said. "I'll call you in the morning to confirm the drop."

"Cool."

After Tony hung up, Doyle nodded to Anita. "Time to hit the road."

Anita turned the key in the ignition. Over the noise of the warming engine, she said, "You didn't answer my earlier question: do you wanna eat first before we return to Jasmine's?"

"I'll catch a burger on the way there," Doyle replied.

Then he remembered the food he'd left behind in the lab, with those two roaches wandering over it like intrepid explorers. The image filled him with disgust and effectively killed his appetite.

He shook his head at Anita. "Nah, baby, on second thoughts, scratch that. I've changed my mind. Let's just go straight to the party. Hopefully, they'll have some potato chips there."

CHAPTER 8

As Doyle and Anita drove away from the F-Bio buildings, a series of events happening in Laboratory No. 7 were building up to a catastrophe.

Everything started when Dr. Annabelle Cole got up from her desk to retrieve a sheaf of printout papers from one of the drawers built into the table that lined the laboratory's east wall. The drawer was stuck, and Dr. Cole had to tug forcefully on it to open it.

Unfortunately, this just happened to be one of the drawers in front of which Doyle had earlier been sitting, and the effort of opening it up resulted in the dislodging of the package of Agent Orange that Doyle had hidden behind the table.

The package thus fell to the floor. While dropping to the floor, the Agent Orange package also dislodged the ages-old hamburger wrapper, which then tilted and spilled its cockroach residents amongst the Agent Orange.

Of course, Dr. Cole had no idea that any of this was happening. When she'd succeeded in forcing the drawer open, something had loudly snapped inside of it, and the loudness of this noise had easily masked the quieter sound of a plastic bag striking the ground out of sight. She ascribed the rustling sound of the burger wrapper settling to the rustling papers in her hand.

But so it was that the cockroaches in the laboratory ended up inside Doyle's precious Agent Orange.

***

Of course, the cockroaches were flustered by their unexpected drop. At first, they all scrambled about haphazardly, as if pursued by vengeful housewives with brooms and cans of insecticide spray. But after a while, the roaches settled down. The fact that they'd landed in a dark place on the ground helped to calm them.

Most calming of all, however, was the strange and compelling scent coming from the powdery orange chunks that now surrounded them. Though not the smell of rotting food, the smell nonetheless compelled the insects to investigate its source, and soon they discovered that the orange stuff not only smelled good but tasted good as well. In a short while, the entire nest of cockroaches—old and young—were gorging themselves on the strange orange food that was not exactly food.

CHAPTER 9

Dr. Cole worked for a while but found it increasingly hard to concentrate. Finally, she got up from her desk and stretched her legs. A glance at her watch informed her that the time was now a quarter to twelve.

I think I'll work till one o'clock and call it a night, she decided.

Normally, Annabelle Cole would have simply taken the extra work home with her. But tonight, she couldn't do that. Time spent with her daughter Jenny was very precious to her. Dr. Cole knew that if she weakened and took her office work home with her, her mind wouldn't be with Jenny this weekend but rather on these research papers.

She walked over to and stared out of the lab's north window, which faced the Appilachian Mountains. Tonight, with the moon out, the landscape made a gentle upward slope. She sensed more than saw the encompassing trees, which at this close range in daylight seemed to ascend forever.

She'd often suggested to Jenny that they go hiking together.

But Jenny, like most young people, is more interested in shopping and partying and . . . Annabelle smiled. *At least we have a nice relationship as mother and daughter. She's not like some young people who forget about their parents once they enter university and can have all the unrestrained sex the internet promises them.*

Her mind momentarily left her daughter and instead settled on her assistant, Doyle. Annabelle didn't like to admit it, but in some ways Doyle Sanders reminded her of her ex Joe. They had the same sort of devil-may-care look in their eyes.

And Joe used to leave food lying all around the place, too, she thought with a gentle laugh.

Then, her mind became business again. She couldn't afford to waste minutes in idle thought when there was work to do. She turned away from the window with its silent night vista and looked back at the work desk.

The only thing to do now is restart the experiment with another test subject. Doyle was right; we should halve the dosage we'll be administering. But we're out of nonaddicted animals, and the fresh batch of rabbits Doyle ordered haven't yet been delivered. . . . Hey, what was that sound?

The sound in question had come from the opposite end of the laboratory.

No, Dr. Cole thought on reconsidering; the sound hadn't come from the far end of the laboratory, where the agent-orange-addicted rodents scrambled about or slept in the cages. But it must have been done. The row of animal cages was the only logical source of the rustling noise she'd heard.

But it sounded like it came from . . .

In fright, Dr. Cole stared over at the drawer she'd earlier battled to force open.

Yes, the noise sounded like it came from over there.

This conclusion upset Dr. Cole. Because it sounded like a rat had made the noise. And Dr. Annabelle Cole detested rats in their free, unrestrained state. Caged, they made great test animals, but they were nasty things if allowed to run free.

Subconsciously detouring past the suspicious drawer, Dr. Cole headed towards the animal cages, looking to see if any of the animals had escaped. That would be very bad. Very bad indeed. But by the time she'd reached the middle of the lab, she could see that all of the crack-addicted rodents were all in their cages.

She looked back towards the drawer. But no further noise had come from that area of the lab, a fact that she should maybe have considered suspicious, as it might mean that a rat was hiding over there and was trying to avoid her noticing it.

Suddenly, Dr. Cole felt a strong need to urinate. She left the lab and hurried to the restrooms down the hallway.

I'll kill Doyle, if he's attracted rats into my laboratory, Dr. Cole thought as she went.

Behind her, the noises issuing from behind the table resumed.

CHAPTER 10

Of course, the noise that Dr. Cole had heard wasn't rats at all, but instead the cockroaches that had accidentally fallen into the package of Agent Orange.

Most of the package's orange content had been consumed by the insects.

By now, the cockroaches in Lab 7 had begun mutating. The mutation process had begun slowly but was now proceeding rapidly.

The most noticeable thing was that the roaches were growing larger. From their initial size of about a flattened fingertip in length, several of them were now already fist-sized.

Of course, the larger the bugs became, the larger their appetites became. The package that had contained the Agent Orange now lay shredded beyond recognition beneath the table, with what remained of the orange narcotic scattered along the wall. The roaches took their time with eating these chunks which now tasted delicious to their transformed appetites.

And the more Agent Orange they consumed, the larger they became.

As the roaches grew in size, their increasing appetites now spread to encompass living flesh. The bodies of the animals in the cages at the end of the lab now smelt delicious and appetizing to them. So, too, did the body of the human woman who'd walked past them.

In the past, the instinct of self-preservation would have prevented the roaches from contemplating an attack on a human being. And a lingering thread of that instinct was what had prevented them from revealing themselves to Dr. Cole as she strode past their hiding place.

Or maybe the roaches were simply exhibiting a new trait: the caution of the predator.

These particular roaches had now mutated, transformed, or evolved into something far beyond the normal; in a sense, they were now alien creatures with largely alien motivations and hunger. They could have fallen from space in a science fiction novel; this was how different the roaches had now become.

Something else developing in the cockroaches was the concept of ANGER.

The final transformation was that all the roaches, from the littlest to the largest, developed huge glowing orange eyes.

At the rate that their size and appetites had developed it was no wonder that all of the Agent Orange the package had contained was soon gone.

The drug was finished, but the roaches' unnatural appetite remained.

CHAPTER 11

After relieving herself in the bathroom and washing her face, Dr. Cole felt a lot better. In the interim—meaning while she'd been sitting on the toilet—she'd decided she'd simply been imagining the presence of uncaged rats in her laboratory.

Though I wouldn't put it beyond that slacker Doyle to accidentally ferry a rat here from home. Judging from the way the young man leaves things lying about in the lab, his home must be absolutely filthy. And that girlfriend of his. She seems neater, but if she's hanging around Doyle, her tidiness must just be a pose.

Dr. Cole drank some water, swirled it around in her mouth, spat it out again, and then left the rest room. It was now half an hour past midnight. Another hour or two of work, and she'd be prepared to call it quits for the weekend. Walking past the other empty labs depressed her somewhat.

With the exception of Security, everyone else in the building left for home and family hours ago, and here I am still . . .

But she didn't spend too much time thinking this way. The moment Dr. Cole walked into her laboratory, she sensed something was wrong. The difference was unmistakable. During the ten or so minutes she'd been away, the atmosphere in the lab had somehow altered.

What is it now? she wondered. *Ten minutes ago, I was hearing things, and now, I'm feeling as if . . .*

But she couldn't put how she felt into words. There was just something in the air now, a factor that hadn't previously been there.

She looked over at the animal cages. They, too, seemed to sense it. Uncharacteristic for them, the caged furry drug addicts were quiet, all of them looking entranced. All of them had retreated to the rear of their cages and were pressed up against the bars back there.

40

They're frightened, Dr. Cole suddenly realized. *But frightened of what? What could possibly scare these little monsters into this state? They look like they're scared of being . . . eaten.*

It was just after thinking this that Dr. Cole ducked out of the way of the football that came whizzing through the air at her. She'd caught the object's motion out of the corner of her eye just in time, or it would have hit her right in the face.

The ball fell to the floor, and Dr. Cole quickly looked around to see who had thrown it. She felt relief when she realized that Doyle had played a prank on her.

But why throw a football at me . . . I could've been badly hurt.

And she quickly realized that Doyle wasn't in the lab. *He can't be. The kid left two hours ago with Anita. I heard them drive off.*

This thought was what made Dr. Cole spin around to get a proper look at the 'football.'

Oh, my dear God . . . what the Hell?

She realized how mistaken she'd been. She understood that her mind, unable to accept the impossibility of what she had actually noticed, had rationalized the oddity into something commonplace.

What Annabelle Cole had imagined as a pigskin oblong was actually alive. It had six segmented legs, a spreading wing case on its back beneath which gossamer wings rustled, and, worst of all, bright orange eyes.

A football-sized cockroach with glowing eyes, eyes that could only have resulted from its consuming an excess of Agent Orange.

Dr. Cole felt like the world was spinning around her. If she'd hated regular-sized roaches, this one utterly terrified her. Now she understood why the animals all seemed terrified. They didn't understand that locked in their cages like they were, they were safe from the fucking creature.

Not like me! I'm right out in the open with it.

She knew that had she not just returned from the toilet, she'd have pissed herself from fright.

The giant cockroach took a step towards her, and she backed away from it. She wanted to turn and run, but what if it flew and landed on her back? Or worse still, became tangled up in her hair? Once, when she was ten years old, a live cockroach had gotten tangled up in her hair and ended up inside the rear of her dress. She'd screamed herself silly before her parents ripped the dress off of her, and she'd had nightmares for days afterwards.

So, there was no way that Annabelle Cole was turning her back on this little monster. And a monster it really was. She continued to back away towards the door. Once she was outside of her lab, she'd be safe.

All I need to do is get outside and lock the door behind me. The bugs can't get out and I can safely send the cavalry in after it. This is what comes of Doyle's messy habits.

She was thinking slowly to calm herself, because otherwise she'd begin panicking and once that happened, she'd begin screaming. Annabelle didn't think insects were sensitive to loud noise per se, but she knew they were very sensitive to vibrations . . . and she didn't want to alarm these ones.

Still, she wished she could scream for Security. Or at least call them. But her cellphone lay across the room on her desk and she was currently trying to exit the lab, not make her way further inside it.

The cockroach on the floor rubbed its mouth parts together and then took a few steps forward, and Annabelle retreated further away from it. She prayed it wouldn't become airborne again. She whimpered when a second cockroach, this one smaller in size, but with proportionately massive orange eyes, stepped out behind the first.

Then, realizing she didn't know how far behind her the door was, Annabelle glanced back.

What she saw horrified her. Two more giant orange-eyed cockroaches had blocked her escape. They stood there in front of the shut doorway like security personnel.

When she looked forward again, she realized that looking away from the original pair of cockroaches had been a mistake. The smaller of the two was now airborne and was flying directly at her.

With her escape route cut off, Annabelle realized she had nothing left to lose by screaming. So, she attempted to do so, but the moment she opened her mouth, the airborne cockroach rammed right into it.

Annabelle suddenly found herself with a mouthful of cockroach. Revolted, feeling like she was going to puke herself to death, she reached up and grabbed the horrible creature. She got a firm hold of its rearmost set of legs, but they were spiky and cut her hands. Still, she held on; she had no options.

And meanwhile, the cockroach was trying to work its way further into her mouth.

Annabelle wished she'd faint. She could feel the giant insect's head twisting and turning inside her mouth, and she was fighting not to instinctively defend herself against the nauseating intrusion by clamping her teeth down behind the roach's head at the junction with its thorax. She's seen too many splattered roaches to dare attempt opening this one up with her teeth; no way did Annabelle want that yellow mess that bugs made when they burst open inside of her mouth.

Instead, while pulling on its legs and trying not to vomit, she tried to spit the bug out.

The roach suddenly bit down on her tongue. Now, Annabelle had blood streaming out of her mouth also. She stood there confused by the unexpected pain, while blood spilled down the front of her lab coat. She tottered left and right in confusion, shredding her hands by tugging on the cockroach's rear legs, but barely dislodging it because its front two pairs of feet were now hooked into her hair and the fabric of her coat.

In Annabelle's panic she'd forgotten she was dealing with at least four giant cockroaches, not just one. She was reminded of the others when she felt a horrible pain in her left calf. Then she felt another pain, and then felt something snap around her ankle.

It just bit through my Achille's tendon! she thought in a panic, and then lost her balance and crashed down onto the laboratory floor.

And yet, she still felt she was being attacked by an impossibility; as if Doyle had spiked her soda with a hallucinogenic. Science had always theorized that the physics of size-to-weight ratios prevented insects from ever-growing this large.

By now, even if Annabelle had been able to remove the obstruction from her mouth, she'd have been unable to scream. The evil bug had made the most of its location between her lips and, by now, had eaten most of her tongue. And now that Annabelle lay prostrate on the floor and its legs had better purchase, the roach wasted no time in forcing itself fully into Annabelle's mouth. She was a mute witness to this outrage against her will, the fall having knocked her mostly senseless.

Dr. Annabelle Cole barely felt the crackroaches strip away first her skin and then her flesh, eating her body away down to the bones.

And mercifully, she was long dead before they were done with her, having asphyxiated almost immediately the cockroach between her lips had fully crawled into her mouth and blocked her throat.

All the while that the giant bugs were eating the dead scientist, the caged crack-addicted animals watched and waited in terror, scared that they would be next, unaware that, tonight at least, the steel walls of their prisons were insurance against their being consumed by this ravening insect death.

CHAPTER 12

When the crack roaches were done with Annabelle Cole, all that remained of her body was an icky smear on the floor. The giant insect's newly discovered hunger for flesh had extended even to their consuming the dead woman's hair and bones.

The giant roaches were ten in number, with a smattering of smaller cousins around them. Some of the latter were still regular-sized, but most filled the size range between little and large. However, all of the bugs had the same glowing orange eyes—eyes that were no longer faceted, eyes that were alien to life on Earth.

Eating up, Annabelle Cole had merely whetted the giant roaches' appetites. Once the dead woman was gone, the roaches turned their attention to the other living creatures in the laboratory, those trapped in the cages.

But here, the insects' hunger proved no match for stainless steel bars. Still, the caged animals quivered in terror while the giant bugs attempted to find an entry between the steel bars that, until five minutes ago, would hardly have prevented their progress. (Fortunately for the rodents, the smaller insects all waited in the rearguard, deferring to their giant cousins to make the initial breach in the defenses.)

Two of the rabbits died during this process—their brains popping from sheer fright. Unfortunately for the giant roaches though, both of the dead bunnies had been squeezing themselves against the rear bars of their cages when their ends came, and so their corpses couldn't be eaten.

Finally, the giant insects understood that they couldn't break into the cages. And so they backed away and climbed back down to the floor. During this process, one of the largest cockroaches lost its footing and landed on its back. In this position, it was unable to right itself again, and after a while of milling around it, the other cockroaches promptly killed and ate it, savaging it as brutally as they had Annabelle Cole.

After that, they spent some time wandering around the laboratory floor in a state of indecision. They couldn't think as such, but the sheer increase in size that they'd experienced as a result of their transformation/mutation meant that they now had more brain capacity, which equaled more intelligence.

Most of the giant insects milled around the vault in which the Agent Orange was stored.

Their appetite was two-fold: firstly, for the flesh to eat, and then, secondly, for the strange orange substance that had made them what they now were. Their first craving had been appeased for a short while. The second—the unquenchable hunger of crack addiction—was just beginning to rear its head. And if the mutated bugs had no conception of either their addiction's nature or of its intense magnitude, they somehow understood that the tasty orange substance was necessary to their continued wellbeing.

But finally, just as they'd been forced to give up their interest in eating the animals in the laboratory cages, so too did they instinctively realize that they couldn't reach the substance in the shiny box near the wall.

And yet, shining through their mass frustration came a light. One consistent characteristic of an Agent Orange addict was their ability to locate other sources of their preferred narcotic by using their noses. This had proven true for both humans and animals. Across mammalian, reptilian, and even cryptid species, the addict's ability to sniff out nearby Agent Orange was almost as acute as a shark's legendary ability to smell blood in water up to two miles away.

And that same ability now manifested itself in these insects also.

Once they stopped focusing their attention on the laboratory safe, each of the giant cockroaches became aware of the presence of a significant store of Agent Orange some distance away from their current location.

Interestingly, they were also able to quantify the amount of Agent Orange as being much more than either that which currently resided in the lab safe or that which had transformed them.

With that settled, it was a no-brainer for the bugs. As one, they set off in the direction of the cache at the other end of the tantalizing smell. This was an orange rainbow, and the crackroaches desired the pot of gold at its end.

Unable to understand or work the door, the roaches left the lab through the window, which ironically was the same way they'd entered it all those nights ago.

This time, all of the insects made it safely down to the ground outside of the laboratory building. And then, keeping in the darkness and shadows, they made their way out of the F-Bio compound and headed into the surrounding woods, their senses following the beckoning Agent Orange smell.

The mutated roaches also sensed that there was a lot of food—living, warm, throbbing flesh that they could eat—waiting for them in the woods.

Both human and animal flesh.

It filled them with anticipation about their trip.

CHAPTER 13

It was the middle of the night, and Mercedes Richard was finding it impossible to sleep. The air conditioning in her trailer had been bad for weeks, and she'd kept putting off having it fixed.

And tonight, it seemed to have packed up completely. Even with the windows flung open, the bedroom was so hot that she'd been forced awake yet again, this time even more sweaty and sticky than last time.

Doggedly refusing to accept the fact that she wouldn't be able to fall asleep again, Mercedes lay in bed for a while longer, while the unwelcome perspiration beaded on her skin and soaked her nightgown and ran between her breasts and down into her crotch. She really didn't want to get up. She really didn't.

But finally, she grew too uncomfortable lying there in bed and staring at the moon through her windows.

Dammit! she thought as she sat up in bed and flicked the nightstand light on.

The time was 2 a.m. in the morning. Both too early and too late to do anything productive.

She got out of bed and went to get herself a glass of milk.

Mercedes Richard was a middle-aged divorcee who lived alone.

Hey, where's Mr. Grouch?

Mr. Grouch was the family cat. A large white tomcat of an indeterminate breed. Normally, the cat slept in Mercedes's bedroom. She was used to waking up to the sensation of him lying on her legs like a fur warmer, or even lying by her head.

I guess my cat also thinks the night's too hot to hang around in bed. He's gone off looking for some pussycat to play with.

She got out the milk carton from the fridge and filled herself up a glass, and then she wondered what in the hell she was going to do with herself until sleep returned.

Well, I can watch some TV, she thought. *There's bound to be something good on somewhere at this time of the morning.* But a quick look down at herself—her sweat-drenched body—quickly changed her mind. *Oh no, sitting in the living room, even with the fan going, will be torture tonight.*

So, instead, Mercedes decided to go sit outside on the patio for a bit and watch the sky.

Once outside and seated on a comfortable deck chair, sipping her chilled glass of milk, she realized she'd made the right decision. Maybe because of all the trees, there was a great crosscurrent of breezes. Which made her wonder how none of this delightful breeze had blown through her windows.

Oh, dammit. I'll call the air-conditioning company first thing in the morning! I can't believe I put it off for so long.

So, Mercedes sat there. And as the level of milk in her glass went down, she remembered the cat. Maybe Mr. Grouch would want some milk too. But where the hell was the cat?

On other nights when she'd sat outside like this, her white tomcat would join her and she'd pour him a saucer of milk and they'd both drink up and stare out at the surrounding forest with its night noises.

Still no sign of the cat. Mercedes sighed. That likely meant he'd headed over towards the Sleepaway Camp again to search for scraps. Her trailer was right at the far east end of the Lake Placid Trailer Park, and the Sleepaway Campground lay further east but was easily accessible through the woods.

And, it was then, while she stared at the woods, that Mercedes thought she heard a noise.

Mercedes froze on her chair and strained her ears. Something about that noise had sounded both familiar and disturbingly strange.

Yes, the forest always has noises, but that particular sound . . .

She listened and heard it again, and then again. The sound was a faint feline mewling. Something about it set Mercedes's hair on edge.

That's Mr. Grouch! He's gotten himself into some kind of trouble.

Without much thought for her own safety in the woods at night, Mercedes finished the dregs of her milk and then hurried into the house to get her shotgun and a flashlight.

***

Once in the woods, however, she paused and considered the logic of her actions. What if Mr. Grouch had angered a bear or even been bitten by a snake?

And what if the noise she'd heard—because it had stopped now— what if that soft feline whimpering hadn't been Mr. Grouch at all, but some other animal, like maybe a raccoon in distress?

Maybe I should just go back home and wait for the cat. This won't be the first time he's wandered over to the campground in the night.

More than anything else, it was Mercedes's need to occupy herself after waking up that made her proceed into the forest. She'd not heard the sickening sound for a while now, but she knew what direction it had come from.

At the verge of the forest, she paused and looked back over at the trailer park. Just about every trailer in sight had its lights off. She looked down at her shotgun.

Do I really wanna wake everyone up in the middle of the night for no good reason?

Sighing, Mercedes walked into the greenery, and the forest swallowed her up.

For a few minutes she saw nothing odd. Yes, once or twice the beam of her flashlight reflected the eyes of some woodlands creature that quickly made itself scarce, but that was all.

"Hey, Mr. Grouch, are you in here?" she called out several times. "Hey, Grouchie, it's mommy!"

Normally, that summons would bring the cat running to her. Not tonight, though. Mercedes figured she'd been right in assuming Mr.

Grouch was currently rooting through the Sleepaway Campground's garbage bins.

Okay, so I'll just look around a bit more, and then call it a night. I'm far enough from home as it is.

She looked back at her home, which was now barely visible between the trees, with the trailer park itself a mere mental impression behind it.

Then, on turning around again, her flashlight shone on something startling.

What the hell is that? That's blood!

Now lifting her shotgun to the ready, Mercedes walked cautiously forward to see better.

Oh, my God! Oh, my dear God!

Then she stood and gaped. What her flashlight had initially revealed was a cord of bloody intestines. Tracing the intestines to their source had now revealed Mercedes's missing cat. Not much of Mr. Grouch was left. The white tomcat had been split open and all of his innards consumed, along with his hindlegs. Though his head remained, both of his eyes had been eaten.

Mercedes ran her flashlight back and forth over the destroyed cat. She now felt the first twinges of fear since leaving her trailer. Sure, animals regularly died in the woods, but this pet carcass she was viewing seemed unnatural.

Mercedes now became aware of the disturbing smell in the air. This was a thick and gross smell that wasn't the smell of the forest, damp underbrush, or decaying leaves and fruit. No, this smell was a smell more regularly encountered close to home, like that time when she hadn't emptied the trashcan in her bedroom for a week, and the rotten Chinese takeaway in there had bred cockroaches.

The unnatural smell would have been unsettling enough in the daytime. But now, deep in the woods at night, the smell had Mercedes's nerves on edge. The roach-like smell was so pungent that she was certain a nest of the nauseating creatures wasn't far away.

She fought against her nervousness. She couldn't just leave her cat out here like this.

With tears pooling in her eyes, she thought: *I'm gonna need to get a box from the house and come gather his remains and give him a good burial.*

Despite her devotion to the cat, however, she didn't feel like handling him in his current state. His remains were too messed up and icky; Mercedes wasn't about touching them.

Okay, I'll just use a trowel to move Mr. Grouch . . . what the hell is that?

A pair of orange lamps seemed to be shining close to her feet. Startled by their appearance, seemingly from nowhere, Mercedes shone her flashlight towards them. Then she gaped in disbelief at what she was seeing.

No, that's impossible!

But the presence of the giant bug beneath the leaves explained the pervasive roach smell in the woods. And the fact that the bug's head was covered with blood explained exactly why Mercedes's beloved cat now looked like a misshapen white-black-and-red Persian rug.

But why were the insect's eyes huge and orange and almost seemed to be popping out of its head? Mercedes Richard had no answer to that puzzle.

The sight of the giant cockroach almost scared Mercedes shitless. She knew that, theoretically, bugs couldn't get this big. She'd read online that size-to-weight considerations restricted how large invertebrates could grow.

But then rage filled her, and she swung her shotgun up to shoot the monster cockroach.

But before she could get a shot off, she heard the swishing of leaves overhead. This delayed her and made her swing her flashlight up to see what was up there.

Shit!

More cockroaches were falling down on her. The bugs landed on her like dark brown rainfall. In instinctive revulsion, Mercedes dropped her shotgun and tried brushing them off. Then panic overcame her, and she fled off through the woods to get away from them. However, the giant cockroaches clung tightly to her, not giving her a moment's succor.

In her blind terror, Mercedes headed not towards home but deeper into the woods, towards the Sleepaway Campground. She couldn't see; the roaches were crawling all over her face. She could also feel them eating her, biting through her nightgown and skin, and tunneling into her body.

She screamed for help, but only once, because when she opened her mouth to do so, one of the roaches crawled onto her tongue. She spat it out again and clenched her teeth tightly.

And the smell of them was in her nostrils; that horrible reek like the basement of an old house where a dog had rotted away.

Finally, Mercedes went blind as the swarming roaches ate her eyes out of her head. She felt her eyes pop and bleed and strange mouth parts probing around inside her eye sockets. Insects fed while clinging to her face with legs like razors, and now she ran in a state of internal darkness through the external darkness.

However, Mercedes wasn't done yet. In desperation, she swatted and beat at the bugs. Several of them splatted to mush beneath her blows, but the rest had her good. She streamed with blood and gore, some of it hers, the rest belonging to her attackers.

A bug slit its way into her belly and bit into her innards. She attempted another scream, but then shut her mouth quickly, just in time to prevent a second insect intrusion.

By now, Mercedes Richards was exhausted. Having somehow escaped knocking herself out against a tree while running blind, or even falling into the nearby river, she'd now literally run herself into the ground.

In the middle of a sprint, Mercedes suddenly staggered to a halt and, now half-mad with terror from her blindness and the creatures eating her alive, she slumped down to the floor.

It might even be considered ironic that by the time Mercedes's stamina and fighting spirit gave out, she'd largely rid herself of the bugs. But by now, she was out of her mind and lay trembling on the ground as if she was waiting for the rest of the giant bugs to catch up to her. Which they now did, scuttling out from beneath the greenery, with the sound of their clacking mandibles increasing their prey's madness.

Mercedes's fall crushed one of the largest roaches to death. But the others killed and ate her just the same.

CHAPTER 14

Once the mutated cockroaches had finished eating up Mercedes Richards, they resumed their journey through the forest towards the distant beckoning smell of Agent Orange.

The human woman had not even figured in their plans. While traversing the forest, they had eaten sufficient wildlife, including birds slumbering in their nests (which was how the roaches had gotten up in the tree over Mercedes's head).

But then the woman turned up, and the bugs left their other feeding and concentrated on her instead. And she had been as delicious as the woman they'd eaten back at the building, in the room with the strange smells and caged food they'd been unable to reach.

But now, with mostly full bellies and the strange desire that the distant orange delicacy caused, the roaches hurried forward.

Along the way, they killed and ate parts of a few more animals that didn't get out of the way quickly enough. Then suddenly, they were outside the forest and staring at a wide and bare expanse.

The roaches had arrived at the Sleepaway Campground parking lot.

Here, the bugs paused for a while, swaying on their segmented legs in a conflicted state. Their problem was twofold:

First of all, they could smell delicious human food nearby, amidst the trees. This food was plentiful and grouped at more than one place, and even had the advantage of not being in an active state. But they had all eaten well on the trip here, and so their hunger was minimal. And even if that wasn't the case, they could now sense that they were very close to the end of their quest for the smell that had attracted them this way. In the bug's collective thinking—with their increased size and brain capacity, they may even have developed a rudimentary hive mind—the human food could wait; investigating the delicious smell was the more pressing concern. Still, ignoring the human flesh upset them.

Their second problem concerned the body of water in their path. Yes, the strange orange food was nearby, but to reach it, the insects would have to cross the Tygart Valley River, which scared them immensely. Cockroaches dreaded and avoided large expanses of water. Like the majority of insects, they couldn't swim and instinctively understood that getting swamped in wetness was a death sentence.

But now, here they were, faced with their worst fear. Worse still, most of the roaches were by now too large and heavy to fly distances longer than a few yards. Even the lightest ones amongst them had full bellies, which had now increased their weight. Additionally, the small roaches acceded to the decisions of the larger ones.

So, for tonight at least, taking to the air was very much out of the question.

But unwilling to be dissuaded this close to the end of their quest, the giant roaches walked across the parking lot anyway. There was no way they could turn back now. At this near distance, the spell of Agent Orange was upon them, almost an additional brain that compelled them to locate it.

While crossing the parking lot, they made a strange sight—like a group of radio-controlled toy cars without the kids to control them. They scuttled quickly past the campers' parked vehicles and off of the parking lot gravel again, back onto the grassy verge on its other side that bordered the river.

They paused there and, while terrified by the river, began searching along its banks for a way to cross it.

Working like this, the roaches soon discovered the bridge at the far west end of the campground. This bridge smelt of new, freshly worked wood. In an excited flurry of limbs and glittering chitin, they hurriedly crossed to the opposite side of the river.

From here on, locating what they sought was simple. Agent Orange was in the last cabin along the river bank.

Like a flood of mud, the roaches swarmed down to the cabin. Unlike the bridge, this building seemed long abandoned. It was just the sort of place a cockroach would consider home, even without the added attraction of that smell, which was tantalizingly close now, so close that the roaches, not understanding that they were having crack withdrawal symptoms, felt themselves entering a frenzy.

The cabin door was shut, but their persistent search for an entrance into the building soon paid off. Around the back of the house, the roaches found an unlocked window, which, once forced open, granted all of them access into the house.

The interior doors were all open, and once inside the cabin, the monster roaches soon found the cache of Agent Orange that had drawn them out here.

And in subdued reverence and awe, the roaches began to feed.

A few of them died right there and then, in rapturous ecstasy, and were eaten up by the others. But most of the remaining two dozen or so roaches ate Agent Orange to their heart's content.

The fact that this cache of Agent Orange had a faint human scent to it, which matched a similar scent to that which they'd eaten at the F-Bio lab, wasn't lost on them either.

CHAPTER 15

Saturday morning.

Doyle Sanders opened his eyes and then rolled over in bed. A glance at the clock on his nightstand revealed the time to be 11 a.m.

Shit! It's really late.

But he already knew why he was waking up so late. Last night at Jasmine's had been one hell of a party. He and Anita hadn't gotten in till 5 a.m.

He glanced over at Anita. She was still fast asleep, lying on her belly, fully clothed amidst the disarrayed sheets. Doyle was fully clothed, too. Both of them had been too exhausted to get undressed when they'd gotten back home. They'd simply pulled their shoes off and laid down in bed. No sex, just a chaste goodnight/good morning kiss.

Smiling at how funny that scene had been, Doyle got out of bed and went to pee.

When he came out of the bathroom, he sat down on the edge of the bed and tried to ignore his hangover and work out his itinerary for the day.

Okay, so first I've gotta head out to the cabin and pick up the drugs for Tony and his friends. Then, I've gotta deliver them to him. Then I have to buy some insecticide and a few roach motels for the lab. I'm sure the janitor will have some of that shit, but I wanna show the doc how committed to her research I am. . . . yeah, I need to go feed the animals this evening, so if I spray the place myself . . . and then I'll try to retrieve that package of Agent Orange. But the morning stuff depends on when Tony . . . Yeah, I don't know what time Tony's gonna want me to make the drop off, so maybe Anita and I can actually buy our groceries—

His phone rang then. After fishing it out of his pocket, he saw it was Tony and quickly accepted the call.

"Hey, man, what's up?" Doyle said. "I was just about to call you."

"Nothing much. Just a slight change in plans."

Doyle wondered what the change in plans could be. "Okay, so what's the change? Your friends don't want their shit anymore?"

Tony laughed. "As if that were possible. Last night they looked like they'd kill me when I told them about the delay."

"Okay . . . so?"

"Well, you know how you're supposed to bring the stuff over sometime today?"

"Yeah, I'm gonna drive out to the campground in a little bit and then I'll call you back and we can—"

"Don't bother going out there yet. Bobby and Melissa have got it into their heads that they'd like to do a spot of camping this weekend. So, I figured that since you'll be going up to the Sleepaway Campground anyway, we might as well all just meet up there in the mountains. You can supply them their drugs, and afterward, we'll all just have an old-fashioned campout."

Doyle thought on this a bit. "I dunno, bro. I gotta feed the lab animals in the evening."

Tony laughed. "C'mon, it'll be fun. Bring along your girlfriend." Then Tony lowered his voice, like he didn't want someone on his end of the line overhearing what he was saying. "Listen, man, even if you ain't in a camping mood, do this for me as a favor. I'm sort of scared to be alone with these two once they get cracked up on that Agent Orange shit of yours. Sharon's gonna be with me, but you know what I mean . . ."

The urgent tone in his voice made Doyle laugh. "Okay, man, I'll see what I can do. I'll discuss it with Anita once she wakes up."

"Alright, bro," Tony said, with some relief in his voice. "Call me back once you guys finalize things."

Tony hung up, and next, Doyle felt a soft female hand on his shoulders.

"I'm awake now," Anita said from behind him. "What were you going to discuss with me?"

After turning around and kissing her, Doyle quickly explained about the change in plans.

"So, what do you think?" he asked afterward. "Are you up for some camping fun this weekend?"

She thought a bit and then nodded. "Sure, why not? The campground is near your office, so we can just drive over there later to feed the animals. And maybe you'll even be able to retrieve the original Agent Orange package you lost yesterday. That way, your emergency stash will be intact again."

Then she looked worried. "Just one thing bothers me about this."

"Which is?"

Anita wagged a finger pointedly in the air. "Well, how do we know that this change of plans isn't a setup? That cabin of yours is right at the end of the campground. Perfectly isolated. Which makes it the perfect place for someone to ambush us both, take the drugs, and shoot us both dead."

Doyle nodded worriedly. "Yeah, I've been thinking about that myself since I got the call." Then he smiled. "But let's not get paranoid. Tony wouldn't do that to me ever."

"You don't know that for certain. Greed makes people act strangely."

"My point exactly. In this case, Tony wouldn't dare kill me. At the moment, he's my main connection for moving the orange I produce. I'm the only chemist who can make the stuff. If he knocks me off, who's gonna make him rich?"

Anita nodded slowly to this. "Okay, let's assume you're right, and for whatever reason, you can trust Tony. How about those other two? From what you've just told me, the pair of them are hardcore crack addicts." She frowned, leaned against him, and sighed. "Honey, I'm saying we need to be careful. If we get killed and buried out there, no one's gonna find our corpses for months."

Doyle thought she was being melodramatic, but he leaned forward and opened the top drawer of his nightstand.

Holding the revolver it contained up to the light, he smiled at his girlfriend.

"Don't worry about that, baby," he said with a cold smile. You and I are going to take proper precautions."

Anita began laughing. She kissed Doyle, and the two of them soon stripped off their clothes and got down to making fervent midday love.

CHAPTER 16

That Saturday morning found park ranger Gary Bentley in a good mood.

He'd woken up on the right side of the bed as it were, made love to his wife Charlotte, and then she'd treated him to a hearty breakfast.

Gary Bentley's good mood had lasted all the while he'd been making his rounds of the eastern camping trails. But happy though he was, he suspected it wouldn't last. Something was bound to happen to screw up his good mood.

Things went sour at about 1 p.m. in the afternoon.

Just when Gary was thinking that he'd walk back to his ranger truck and get out his lunch, he saw a blood trail leading off the side of one of the western camping trails that bordered the Sleepaway Campground parking lot.

Thinking that maybe a raccoon or squirrel or even a deer had hurt itself on something and crawled off to die nearby, Gary stopped and crouched for a better look. Whatever had happened here had clearly occurred hours ago; he could tell from the dried blood on the nearby grass. Clearly just a regular animal mishap. And yet, something struck him as odd here.

Not knowing what to expect, Gary Bentley stepped off the camping trail and followed the blood trail to see where it led.

When he came upon the remains of the dead animal, he stood and scratched his chin in puzzlement.

Wow. What the hell kind of an animal did this to this coon?

The raccoon seemed to have been skinned, and its skin was left behind along with its head. That was what it looked like. It still had its head and one rear paw left, but everything else that its body had contained—muscles, bones, entrails—all of that was missing. On closer examination, even the act of leaving the raccoon's skin behind seemed to be something of an afterthought for this unknown predator: the discarded fur had long tears in it that didn't strike Gary as being the work of regular claws.

Worst of all, the head/animal skin mess stank. Gary tried to place the odor but failed. Yes, it was partly composed of decaying meat, but something else was mixed in with it.

Even skunks don't reek this much. It'd take like a million roaches for anything to stink this bad.

Gary didn't understand why the cockroach similarity had come to his mind, but that was the closest similarity he found.

For a short, while, he stood there staring at the raccoon's remains, then he looked around for animal tracks that would indicate what sort of predator had savaged the raccoon-like this.

He found nothing he could make sense of except at one bare patch of nearby forest floor, where he noticed a set of shallow indentations in the soil like someone had been digging a stick into the ground. The marks were initially puzzling until he decided they must be the result of a bird's digging for worms. More than one bird, from the looks of it.

He was just about to return to the raccoon's carcass when his eye fell on another blood splatter. This crimson splash lay vertical on a tree trunk.

Now starting to feel a little bothered, Gary hurried over there to see what he'd find. Then he once again stood and stared.

What the hell?

This time, the animal carcass was that of a large snake. About half of the serpent's body was missing, except for its bones, that was. Without the slightest concession to logic, the snake had been opened up in a myriad of places.

What puzzled Gary the most here was that he recognized the snake species from its marking. It was a Northern Copperhead, one of the state's two venomous snake species.

And we don't have any darn mongooses here in West Virginia. So, what the hell fucked this snake up like this?

It seemed an impossible question to answer. Just about any mammal, Gary could imagine, would have steered well clear of a Copperhead. Gary didn't know of anything that considered such a venomous creature as prey.

But once again, there was that same smell in the air—fainter this time, but discernible once you had an idea to look for it.

Gary got out his cell phone and took pictures of both dead animals. It was something to ask a zoologist about.

An idea occurred to him then. After creating an imaginary line connecting the two dead animals, he set off in the direction their killer might have been moving. One direction would lead back the way he was coming from; the other would lead towards the campground parking lot, and his truck and his lunch. Hunger made the decision for him.

Motivated by curiosity, Gary strode off through the forest in search of the elusive predator. It was grasping at a thread, really, as he knew the animal could have gone in the other direction.

But he soon discovered his hunch was right. A short while later, he found another carcass, this one another partially consumed raccoon. He photographed the grisly remains and kept going. Maybe fifty yards further on, he came upon yet another dead animal. However, this time, he had no idea what species the dead creature was; its head and limbs were gone, and then there was just a random mess scattered amidst the woods.

Like it had eaten its fill and had now begun playing with its food, Gary thought. The 'buggy' smell was still present but well diluted now because the forest ended barely five feet away, and breezes would easily reach in here.

Then he noticed something else on the ground: a bug of some kind. It was quite large, but like the dead carcasses, it had been partially consumed. All of its head and most of its thorax were missing. There simply wasn't enough left of it to identify its species.

He made a mental note to research on what kinds of insects frequented this forest. This one might be some migratory type he'd never seen before.

Before heading to his car to get his lunch, Gary stood at the edge of the forest and considered some things.

The animal that ate those other animals must've come out of the forest at this point, he told himself. *And in that case, it either went back the way it came; or it crossed the parking lot into the forest on the other side. Whatever it is, it's dangerous, but maybe it's scared of people. So far today, I've had no reports of anything attacking the campers overnight, so it most likely went back to its hole on this side.*

From where he stood at the edge of the parking lot, the Tygart Valley River was a silver line off which the sun glittered.

Or did it cross the river? Gary wondered, staring coldly at the line of cabins on its opposite side. *And if it did, what the hell would it be looking for on the other side?*

Then he stared up at the mountains in the background and grinned to himself.

"Maybe it strayed down here from up there, and now it's returned home again. A young bigfoot or something cryptid like that."

Laughing at how silly that sounded, even to himself, Gary Bentley walked over to his ranger pickup truck and got out his lunch.

CHAPTER 17

It was late evening when Doyle and Anita arrived at the Sleepaway Campground. Because this was a last-minute arrangement, there had been all sorts of things to handle first. Including packing their stuff and buying food and drinks.

"But here we are finally," Anita said, steering their car into the campground parking lot where the others were waiting for them.

Tony and another young man were lounging against Tony's brown SUV, and as Anita pulled up beside it, Doyle caught sight of Tony's girlfriend, Sharon, chatting to a redhead inside the SUV.

Anita parked, and they both got out.

"Hey, bro, you finally made it," Tony greeted them.

"Not our fault, dude. Seeing as this was a last-minute thing, we had lots of already-planned stuff to handle first."

"Including buying food and beer," Anita added. "Lots of beer."

"Yeah, it's time to par-tee!" Tony said with a fist pump.

"Business before pleasure," the other guy said, then extended his hand to shake Doyle's. I'm Bobby." He pointed to the young redhead woman emerging from the SUV. And this is my girl Melissa."

Bobby and Melissa were both skinny, clearly from their drug addiction. At first impression, the pair seemed nice enough, but Agent Orange addicts were Doyle's bread and butter, and he knew that, in this case, appearances were completely deceptive. This seemingly harmless couple would become murderously violent in seconds if anyone interfered with their next fix.

Doyle had seen this play out too many times to ever feel relaxed around those addicted to Agent Orange.

Thank heavens I thought to bring the gun along, he thought.

"I'm Doyle, and this is Anita," he replied to the other man's introduction.

"Delighted to meet you both," Bobby said.

Also, meeting for the first time, Anita shook hands with Tony's girlfriend, Sharon. Sharon was small and cute.

There was some silence while a family of four emerged from the nearby forest and climbed into their SUV, parked two cars away.

"Hey, man, you got our stuff?" Melissa asked once the family's SUV had reversed out of parking, her body giving just the slightest impression that she had the shakes.

Doyle nodded at her. "You wanna get high, lady? I got your supply. Just cool it till I get the stash out."

"Great, man." Bobby slapped Doyle on the back, and Melissa grinned. Bobby's and his girlfriend's eyes were noticeably tinted orange. As orangeheads, that was normal enough.

"So, where's this cabin of yours at?" Tony asked.

Doyle gestured across the river. "Last cabin . . ."

Tony looked confused. "And it's safe? No one comes out there?"

Doyle laughed. "It's a family residence. My grandpa built it about fifty years ago, long before this campground was built. I'm not sure if we own part of the land around here or not; Gramps was always vague on that score, and my dad seemingly has no idea, either. But either way, the town authorities don't seem to care, so . . ." Doyle shrugged. "We can spend the night in the cabin, or you guys can pitch a tent outside. There's a lovely concealed stretch by the river."

"Sounds great," Bobby said, and Doyle now noticed that his voice was a bit shaky, too. The guy was holding himself together, but for how long?

The sooner I get these two sorted out, the better. Then we can relax and enjoy the weekend.

Doyle nodded to Tony. "Let's each unload our stuff and head over there," he said. Then turned to Anita. "Baby, I'll carry the beer and our backpacks. Please remember to leave the cans of bug spray behind when you're getting the food bags out of the backseat."

"Bug spray?" Tony looked amused. "What you doin' with bug spray?"

Doyle sighed. "We've got a minor roach infestation at the office, but the doctor's begun giving me grief over it. I was going to discuss it with the janitor guy, but then I decided to handle it myself instead. Once we're all settled in, I'll head over there to feed the animals and also . . ."

Tony nodded and everyone began the task of offloading their camping supplies. Then, when they all had as much as they could carry on this first trip, they set off through the trees that lined the river bank to the bridge near Doyle's cabin.

"You know, I don't recall any bridge being down this way the last time I was camping up here," Sharon said.

Doyle nodded at Tony's girlfriend. "You're right, there wasn't; the city just built this bridge last month. They want easier access to the mountain trails for both campers and rangers."

Anita laughed. "In the old days, we'd have crossed the river up near the parking lot and then made our way down along the river bank on that side."

Doyle laughed. "I much prefer having *my own* bridge. That way, I've much less interference in my business."

He winked at Anita, and she grinned back. "Or *our* pleasure, baby," she added.

With everyone laughing, they crossed the bridge.

CHAPTER 18

Gary Bentley was back home, but restless. His wife Charlotte was in the kitchen getting dinner ready; he could hear her humming in there as the smell of cooking steak floated out into the living room.

Gary had felt happy and calm until Charlotte had gotten the steaks out of the freezer. The sight of them brought back the memory of those weird animal remains. Since then, he'd been searching online for a clue as to what sort of animal had made that mess. It didn't help either that he vaguely remembered the 'buggy' smell that surrounded the ruined carcasses.

He had no luck googling the culprit. Finally, he got to his feet, walked into his study, and pulled out his shotgun.

Silently, so Charlotte wouldn't see he had the weapon on him, he padded swiftly past the kitchen door. Only when he'd safely concealed the weapon by the front door did he return to the kitchen.

"Hey, honey," he told Charlotte. I've got to dash out for five minutes. I need to get something from the store."

She looked around, sweet and homely in her apron. "Can't it wait till later? Dinner's almost ready."

He shook his head. "Won't take me but a minute. But if I get delayed, just leave mine in the oven for me."

He ran off before she could make further inquiries as to what was going on.

Five minutes later, Gary was zooming down the highway toward the Sleepaway Campground.

He had a hunch that whatever that strange creature was, it was going to make another appearance tonight. And he intended to be right on the spot when it showed up.

CHAPTER 19

The interior of the cabin was clean enough, but . . .

"This place smells really weird," Melissa said after Doyle flicked on the lights in the front room, and the generator out back of the cabin sputtered to life. The young redhead dropped her bags, straightened up again, wrinkled her nose, and added: "Almost like you have a roach infestation or shit."

Doyle could smell it, too. He dropped his and Anita's backpacks. "I'll open up the windows," he said.

As he walked through the cabin— living room, bedroom, kitchen, bathroom, store—he pondered the smell. The cabin hadn't smelt like this the last time he'd been here, which was two weeks ago.

Maybe it's to do with a change in the weather, mold or mildew, or some shit like that.

He opened up the cabin windows, but the icky smell stubbornly persisted. Luckily, he found a half-full can of air freshener in the bathroom. He walked back out into the front room with the can held in front of him, sweetening the air as he emerged.

"Ta-da!" he said to the others. "This should help a bit."

Melissa was helping Tony open up the front room windows. Bobby was slumped on the front room couch. Doyle realized he'd better get them their drugs quickly to avoid a scene.

"Hey, let's sort out the business before pleasure," Tony said. Where's the stuff you've got in here?"

Doyle nodded over at Anita. "Go fetch the orange, baby."

"Okay, baby." She nodded and walked off into the kitchen.

Still wary of being double-crossed by Tony and his friend, Doyle, and Anita had worked out this strategy on their drive over here. Anita would get the drugs, while Doyle, appearing unconcerned about the others, would keep an eagle-eye view on them all, with his fingers not straying far from his revolver. The gun was now in the right rear pocket of his pants, concealed by his overhanging shirttails.

"Bring out one of the packs in there; leave the other three where they are," he'd told her. "Of course, after this weekend, we're gonna need to find another place to hide the stuff."

"Man, I'm fucking hungry," Sharon told Tony while they awaited Anita's return.

Tony pulled Sharon close. "Well, we've lots of food and drink, though Doyle and I will need to go back to the car for the beer cooler."

Then Anita walked back out into the front room. She looked confused.

"What's the matter?" Doyle asked her, with a sinking feeling in his belly.

"The drugs . . . they're all gone!"

"What?" almost everyone in the cabin asked at once.

"I'm serious, baby," Anita said. "There aren't any drugs in the kitchen anymore."

"But that's impossible!" Doyle shouted in dismay. Forgetting his and his girlfriend's initial strategy, he ran out of the front room, almost shoving Anita out of the way in his haste to see what she was talking about.

She'd told him the truth. The plastic packages of Agent Orange had been stored in a box behind the fridge. Now that box lay in pieces on the floor in front of the fridge, and all of the orange narcotic it had contained was gone.

Tony had just joined Doyle beside the tattered carton. The evidence was clear; something or someone had gotten in here and stolen the Agent Orange.

"But how could someone steal it?" Doyle asked himself aloud. "You guys all saw me open up the front door." Then he recalled that one of the bedroom windows had been partially open.

Aw, shit! he thought. *I really did have a break-in!*

"What the hell! No drugs again!" Melissa was still outside in the living room, but the redhead's voice sounded close to panic.

"No, no, no!" Bobby's voice joined hers in chorus. "I'm getting really angry now, sweets. I feel like I could kill someone."

Great. Just great, Doyle thought.

He and Tony were still squatting down near the tattered box, with Anita bending over them.

"What the hell are we gonna do now?" Tony whispered to Doyle in a very worried tone of voice. "You can hear them yourself. Any moment now, they might turn violent on us."

"Yeah, the crazies sound like they're about to start running the asylum," Anita added.

"Try to calm them down for half an hour," Doyle whispered back. Then, as earlier planned, I'll drive over to the lab and fetch the original package of Agent Orange I made for them."

"How long should that take?"

Doyle thought on it. "Forty-five minutes at most. I need to feed the lab animals, too."

Tony looked unconvinced. "I dunno, bro. What if Dr. Cole comes back to the lab tonight also?"

Doyle shook his head. "She won't. Her daughter is in town for the weekend. She never lets anything get in the way of spending time with her."

Tony nodded. "Okay then, I'll cover for you, bro. But make it damn fast. I don't like the way those two have gone all quiet out there in the living room. Shit, I should have brought Sharon in here with me"

Doyle listened and realized it was true. Outside in the front room, silence reigned, almost like everyone was dead.

"Guys, there's something weird about this," Anita said above their heads.

Doyle and Tony turned to look up at her. "What do you mean?"

In response, Anita crouched down also and picked up a piece of the ruined carton. "Have a look at this. This doesn't look torn. It looks like it's been *eaten.*"

The two men each picked up a piece of carton and examined it closer. Then, together, the three of them got up to their feet.

"You're right, baby," Doyle said. "An animal did this." He sighed. "Raccoons, most likely. I found one of the bedroom windows open when I went in there."

"Hey, we're wasting time here," Tony whispered. "We need to remember we've got a situation brewing that we need to defuse fast."

"Hold on a bit," Anita said in an urgent voice, waving the tattered strip of cardboard in her hand at the other two. "Guys, I don't think this is the work of a raccoon."

Tony was slowly losing his patience now. "C'mon, girl, what else could've done this? What else could've broken in here and stolen that much of your boyfriend's stash?" He turned his attention back to Doyle. "Listen, bro, I already told you I don't like how those two suddenly went all silent out there. It's a guarantee that they're scheming something evil. And my girlfriend's out there with them."

Doyle looked at Anita. "He's right, baby, we need to—"

She restrained him with a hand on his arm. "Guys, don't you get it? The smell—that mangy smell Melissa mentioned immediately after we stepped through the front door. The smell is thickest in here."

Doyle and Tony looked at each other. She was right. The smell was thickest in the kitchen.

"And there's one other thing," Anita said, before bending out of sight behind the fridge for a moment. When she straightened up again, she was holding something that looked like a rat. She wasn't holding it with her hand, but wrapped in the shred of cardboard she'd been holding onto.

"It's a cockroach," she told them in a disgusted voice. "Ugh! A giant cockroach. But that's not all. Notice anything peculiar about its eyes?"

Both men did—the huge roach had bright orange eyes. Of course, it was dead. It seemed to have died because its body had grown too big for its carapace to cope. In a parody of human stretch marks, the orange-eyed roach was split lengthwise in more than one place, and orange innards bulged out of these cracks.

Doyle was horrified. Even Tony's concern about his girlfriend had suffered a sudden drop in intensity.

"Shit, man!" Tony said. "Agent Orange did this to a damn cockroach."

"I'm shocked myself," Doyle said. "Fucking bugs ate my drugs?"

"Guys, you're missing the point here," Anita said, in a voice that showed she was doing her very best to keep from screaming at them in panic. "And the point is that this huge damn cockroach"—she now flung it away from her—"can't have been the only one that ate up all of the Agent Orange we kept in here. Doyle, that was a whole lot of Agent Orange."

"About five kilos of the stuff," Doyle admitted.

Anita nodded. "Yes, and where's the rest of it?"

Tony looked horrified. "You're telling us that there's more of these things?" He glanced at the monster bug like he'd vomit. "More giant cockroaches?"

Doyle nodded. "I think she's right. It's the only explanation that makes sense. It explains why the box was shredded and . . . Yes, it all makes sense now." The analytical sector of his mind had begun working.

"Fuck making sense of all this, Doyle!" Anita said angrily, now not bothering to whisper. "Listen to me, you two. What I'm getting at is . . . judging from the smell in the cabin, and in here in particular, the roaches are still in the house. They never left." She sighed and gestured first out through the kitchen window, out where night had now completely fallen, then over at the huge dead cockroach on the floor, which, in this motionless state, seemed to be a rubber Halloween decoration. "And in case, you're missing the whole picture, cockroaches are nocturnal. Meaning that if they've been sleeping through the day, they're about to wake up now that it's nighttime. Do you get it now?"

Doyle gulped. "Fuck, we need to get out of here, as fast as we can. We don't want to deal with giant cockroaches addicted to Agent Orange."

Anita nodded. "Yeah. Those insecticide cans in our car won't make the slightest difference to bugs of this size."

Tony was already leaving the kitchen. "C'mon, let's get the hell out of here."

The other two quickly followed him.

"Guys, we've got an emergency situation!" Tony said immediately as he stepped out into the living room. We need to get the hell out of here right away!"

Then he, Doyle, and Anita stopped in their tracks.

Bobby was pointing a gun at them. Behind him, Melissa held a switchblade knife to Sharon's neck.

"Ain't nobody going nowhere," Bobby said in a cold voice. "Not till Melissa and I get our Agent Orange."

Fuck, Doyle thought. *Fuck me sideways!*

CHAPTER 20

"Exactly where do you three think you're going?" Melissa said from behind Bobby.

Doyle winced on, seeing that her eyes were now a bright glowing orange. So, too, were Bobby's.

"Listen, we need to get out of here," he said as calmly as he could, wishing he'd heeded Tony's warning that they needed to attend to Bobby and Melissa before the pair went crazy.

"Out into the living room, all of you," Bobby said. "Hands up where I can see them."

Melissa nodded. "One wrong move from any of you, and it's curtains for missy here." To make her point, she lightly grazed Sharon's neck with her knife, drawing blood.

"Please, let her go!" Tony pleaded. "You don't get it. We've got a situation here. One we didn't plan for."

"Yeah, I agree we've got a situation," Bobby agreed. "And that situation is that our fucking drugs are missing again. And that really pisses me off." He glanced over at Melissa. "How 'bout you, hon? That piss you off or not?"

"I'm mad as hell now," Melissa agreed. "We've paid Tony for our drugs, and once again, he's stiffed us. Personally, I feel like killing him."

Tony gulped. "Listen, I'll refund your damn money. Just let Sharon go, and let's get out of here. I'm telling you, seriously, it ain't safe in here. This cabin may be infested with giant cockroaches."

Doyle nodded. "He's telling the truth. From the looks of things, the damn bugs must've eaten up the Agent Orange I left in here."

At that statement Bobby and Melissa both burst out laughing. Then Bobby walked over to Tony and placed the gun against his forehead.

His entire body was visibly shaking now. "Do I look dumb to you, bro? Do I? Do I? Where's our fucking orange?"

"Hey, baby, get the dealer's gun," Melissa called out.

"Yeah, I almost forgot he had heat on him," Bobby said and shifted the placement of his gun's muzzle from Tony's head to Doyle's.

Fuck this! Doyle's hopes sank when the cold metal touched his head, with death now just a finger-twitch away. And with the way Bobby had the shakes now, he could pull the trigger by accident. He flinched as Bobby lifted his shirt and retrieved the revolver from his back pocket with his free hand.

Bobby stepped back again and handed Doyle's gun to Melissa, who clicked her switchblade shut and put it away, causing both Sharon and Tony to sigh in relief. The danger of Melissa holding her knife to Sharon's neck hadn't been lost on either of them; she had the shakes almost as bad as her boyfriend did.

Melissa then shoved Sharon away from her. "Bitch, go stand with the other double-crossers."

Sharon hurried over to Tony's side. Anita was already huddled behind Doyle, peeking over his shoulder at their friends now turned captors.

"Listen, guys," said Doyle slowly. "You don't want to hurt us. You just want your Agent Orange, and I'm the man to get it for you."

"Shut the fuck up, or I'll fill you with lead right now," Melissa said, pointing the revolver at Doyle. "You ain't about to screw us over again."

"No, no, no, please listen to me," Doyle said, holding up his hands in a pacifying gesture. "Even forgetting the danger here in the cabin for the moment—"

"Hey, asshole, there's no fucking danger in here," Bobby said, his orange eyes bright and distorted in his face. "Stop fucking lying to me!" After shouting this at Doyle, Bobby seemed to lose track of his thoughts for the next few seconds, which he spent wildly pacing the room while banging the grip of his gun against the side of his head.

Nobody said anything, but Melissa watched him with a smile. Finally, Bobby whirled around and walked over to Doyle again. Once more, he placed the gun to Doyle's forehead.

"Okay, I'm listening to what you got to tell us. You got something to say, say it. But if you dare mention giant bugs again, I'll blow your fucking brains out."

Doyle nodded and then said, as calmly as he could manage: "Here's what you're overlooking: We've still got the other batch of dope that I cooked up yesterday over at the lab. I simply need to retrieve it from where it got stuck. Listen, guys, I can drive over there and fetch it for you. At most, it'll take me fifteen minutes to make the return trip."

After suggesting this, he waited. He sensed that they'd reached some sort of turning point—there was insanity in the air, and there was no way he could predict which way the cards would fall. If God was pissed off at him for dealing dope, well then, Bobby might reject his suggestion and shoot them all, and that would be that.

Bobby mused about Doyle's words. Unable to make up his mind, he turned to Melissa. "What do you think, hon?"

"I don't trust him. This is the second time he's screwed with us."

Doyle again raised his hands in a placating gesture. "This has all been a huge misunderstanding. I can get you your drugs, but you're gonna have to trust me."

Bobby laughed. "Trust you? You must be out of your damn mind."

"Listen, I'll go with him," Tony said.

Bobby laughed even louder. "That makes it even worse. I trust you even less than I trust your chemist friend."

"I don't see what the problem is," Anita said. "You'll have both of us girlfriends here as hostages. They're not going to run off and leave us here, are they?"

"No, but one of them could go lie to the cops about a hostage situation," Melissa said.

"How, in the fuck can I go to the police?" Doyle protested. "I'm fucking dealing drugs. At the moment, I'm possibly the most wanted man in this part of the fucking USA."

For the first time, Bobby smiled. "Yeah, you do make a good point. But I still don't trust you two. There's nothing stopping both of you from breaking out a cache of shotguns and coming back to shoot us all up."

"We won't," Doyle said tiredly. "We just want to get this over with. What in hell's name is it gonna take to make you believe that?"

"Okay, here's what we're gonna do," Bobby said while scratching his hair with his gun. I'm going with the chemist to the lab where he works and coming back with the drugs. That way, there'll be no chance of a double-cross."

"Yeah, that's fine with me," Doyle agreed in relief. "Just keep a low profile when we get there, is all I'm asking."

Bobby nodded. "Don't you worry about that? Just get me the Agent Orange, and you'll have no problems."

"Yeah," Melissa said, with a shake of her red hair. "You get us our orange, and our party is gonna resume like nothing ever went amiss here."

"Alright, so that's settled then," Doyle said. "Let's be on—"

"Hey, baby, what if they jump me?" Melissa asked, gesturing at Anita, Tony, and Sharon with Doyle's revolver. "You don't expect me to keep an eye on these three all by myself, do you?"

"Don't worry, hon. They won't be able to jump you," Bobby replied. We're gonna tie 'em up first."

CHAPTER 21

Bobby told Doyle, "Get into the kitchen and find us some rope or duct tape. Whatever we can tie everyone up with."

Doyle nodded, smiled reassuringly at Anita, and then did as he'd been told. As Bobby suspected, there was some duct tape up in one of the kitchen cabinets. Doyle got it out quickly and made to return to the living room.

But then he froze in his tracks.

The giant dead bug Anita found . . . what happened to it? He looked around the kitchen floor. No doubt about it; the bug was gone. A suggestion of what had happened to it might be half of a wing case that lay near the storeroom entrance like something had broken it off the oversized insect's body.

The storeroom door was partly open, and Doyle decided to shut it for safety's sake. But the door wouldn't close, no matter how hard he pulled on it.

"Hey, what's taking you so damn long in there?" Bobby called.

"Coming, man."

After a final tug on the door refused to shut it, Doyle hurried back outside with two rolls of duct tape in his hand.

"I found the tape," he said. "But there's something else, I think you need to know."

Bobby calmly pointed his gun at Anita's head. "One word from you about giant bugs, and *she* gets it. I don't wanna hear that sci-fi shit."

"No, he doesn't. He prefers action flicks," Melissa said.

And so, not wanting to lose his hot girlfriend to a maniac's delusions, Doyle kept his suspicions and worries to himself. All he could think of was hurrying over to the lab and hurrying back again, before anything really went wrong in here. He didn't know anything for sure, but the nasty stench coming from the pantry/storeroom had been intense like nothing he'd ever smelt before, like someone was breeding roaches in there.

Melissa played eeny-meeny-miney-mo with her revolver on the prisoners, then finally pointed to Tony. "Do him first."

"Yeah," Bobby agreed. "Wrists behind his back first, then make his ankles secure too."

Tony didn't protest while Doyle and Anita bound him. But while they were working, he whispered to Doyle. "Man, I don't get it—that fucking smell in the house seems to be increasing."

"Yeah," Anita agreed. "But it appears our two crackheads can't smell it."

"Hey, I heard that," Bobby said. "But I'm in a good mood, so I won't shoot you for it." He nodded at Sharon. "Okay, you're next. Turn around and stretch out your damn hands backward."

Sharon did as she was told. "Don't worry," Doyle whispered to her as he bound her wrists behind her. "I'll drive fast, and hurry back here."

But Doyle never even left the cabin. Because right then, was when Melissa screamed.

CHAPTER 22

It took a while for Doyle to work out exactly why Melissa had yelled. First of all, he gaped at her, and then he realized that she was gaping at something behind him, so he turned around and stared that way, too.

And then he almost shat himself in fear.

A giant cockroach, about the size of a football, was scuttling out of the kitchen door. Even more scary than its giant size was its mutated state—in addition to having giant orange eyes, this abnormally large cockroach had possibly more legs than a millipede.

"What the fuck?" Bobby gasped in horror on noticing the bug, his gun almost falling from his fingers, while Melissa instinctively lifted her legs up onto the couch she was sitting on.

"What the fuck?" Bobby repeated with a look on his face that indicated he thought he was in the grip of some weird hallucination created by his Agent Orange withdrawal.

And now, following after the monster roach came a seeming flood of smaller ones; a few normal-sized, others about fist-sized, but all of their eyes glowing crazily.

When Doyle saw the other bugs, he immediately shoved Anita towards the bedroom. To his mind, this was the only logical direction of flight because the roaches' path of advance led them directly past the front door.

"Go!" he urgently told Anita, "and keep watch at the bedroom door so the bugs don't get inside!"

Doyle's problem now was how to free both Tony and Sharon before the roaches reached them.

Sharon's case was easier. Just like with Tony, Doyle had made her sit down as a prelude to binding her ankles together. But the deed wasn't yet done, so he just had to pull her to her feet and push her after Anita.

"Go!" he told her.

Sharon stumbled off after Anita, but she never made it to the bedroom.

The lead giant bug had temporarily paused its advance, with its long antennae waving side to side as if it were scanning the room. Now, as Sharon attempted to run past it to the safety of the bedroom, the giant cockroach launched itself at her.

The roach moved deceptively fast for its giant size, covering the space between them both and snaring both of Sharon's legs between its hideously mutated and oversized mandibles. Then there was a horrible cracking noise of shattering bones, and Sharon fell sideways to the floor with both of her legs cut completely through at the ankles. One of her severed feet remained upright; the other one fell sideways in the opposite direction to its felled owner.

Sharon lay on the floor halfway to the hallway, jerking in shock from the pain, while her blood jetted from her leg stumps.

The giant roach now dug its mouth parts into Sharon's body and began feeding.

Everyone stared in horror, gaping at what had happened to Sharon. Then Melissa began making a strange keening noise that snapped Doyle out of his own frozen state.

"Give me a hand with getting Tony off the floor!" he shouted at Bobby. "We've not time to untie him; we've got to get into the bedroom!"

Bobby nodded and ran over to help. Melissa had scarcely gotten over whatever panic crisis she was having. She made no attempt to help the men get Tony upright. She was too frightened. More bugs were now pouring out of the kitchen, and several were on their way to the couch. Melissa leaped down from the couch, stomped several cockroaches into mush, and then ran and leaped over both Sharon and the cockroaches that were having her for dinner. She landed safely on the far side of the roaches and hurried on past Anita into the safety of the bedroom.

Doyle and Bobby had now gotten Tony safely to his feet. They were now faced with both an advantage and a disadvantage. The advantage was that Sharon had fallen to the ground in a direct line from the hallway entrance to the front door, meaning the giant roaches had to get past her to reach the side of the room where the three men stood, which delayed them because a good number of the roaches simply didn't bother to proceed beyond feasting on the dead woman.

The disadvantage was that those bugs that did skirt the obstruction were the largest of the lot. One of these was twice as big as the roach that had bitten off both of Sharon's feet. Just like the dead bug Anita had found in the kitchen, the carapace of this enormous cockroach had stretchmark slits in it, inside of which its orange flesh was visible. It still moved, however. Heavily and somewhat painfully it seemed, but with clear purpose to reach and attack them.

"Shoot it!" Doyle told Bobby.

Bobby looked at the gun in his hand like he'd forgotten what it was. "Yeah, yeah, yeah," he said next and fired at the giant cockroach. But either he was a crap shot, or he was simply too nervous to shoot straight, or just possibly his Agent Orange shakes threw his aim completely off, because he didn't hit the giant roach anywhere dangerous. He didn't miss it altogether, but the bullet zinged off the side of its body and instead slammed into the pile of roaches that were making a meal of Sharon.

"Fuck this!" Bobby said and fled for the bedroom. Along the way, he barely escaped, skidding on Sharon's spilled blood, tripping over her, and falling amidst the roaches. But after stomping a couple of them into the rug, he, too, made it through the bedroom door.

That left just Doyle and Tony out in the open with the roaches. In addition to that largest cockroach getting closer to them by the second, with another, almost as large making up distance close behind it, the rest of the floor was quickly filling up with bugs too. It wouldn't be long before there wasn't any free floor space to step in.

In the meantime, Tony wasn't helping matters much. Sharon's death (and watching the mutated insects feasting on her a few yards away) seemed to have drained the willpower out of him. He was mostly dead weight while going in whatever direction Doyle shoved him and seemingly unable to stop staring at his dead girlfriend.

Doyle did the only thing he could. "Hey, listen, man," he told Tony. "I'm gonna untie your feet, and then we're both gonna have to run for it!"

Tony didn't reply, and Doyle got down and got to work. He didn't imagine he'd make it before the giant bug reached them, and he almost didn't. But somehow, he got the strip of duct tape off. (Thank God he'd not made it too tight!)

"Okay, run," he told Tony. "Go!"

Doyle and Tony ran. Possibly seeing more potential dinner escaping them, the bugs ran, too. Doyle made it through the roach gauntlet; Tony didn't.

Doyle almost didn't make it to the bedroom door either. He slipped on something—he later realized it was one of the squashed bugs that either Melissa or Bobby had spattered during their own flight to the bedroom—and found himself on his belly on the hallway floor. Then, when he rolled over onto his back and tried to get up again, a giant cockroach was flying at him with its mandibles clacking fiercely.

Doyle flung up his hands to shield his face.

Then a gunshot resounded, and next, Doyle felt something splat down on his legs. He quickly opened his eyes. The giant bug had fallen on him but was half-burst open and was leaking orange fluids as it lay there on its back on his knees, violently kicking its legs in an attempt to stand upright again.

In total revulsion, Doyle kicked the dying insect away from his body and leapt back to his feet. A look behind him revealed that Bobby had shot the bug out of the air. So, the man had clearly regained his nerve.

"Get the hell inside here!" Bobby and Anita were both gesturing wildly at him.

But Tony? Doyle turned around once more to look for his friend. But he could only make out Tony's legs there on the floor, kicking violently, while the roaches swarmed over him, and jets of his blood squirted through the air.

Those roaches that were still alive were giving Tony and Sharon their full attention, and making no attempt to approach the bedroom door.

Doyle threw up. He could hear Tony groaning in pain, his voice miserable as hell.

"Get your damn ass inside here!" Anita yelled at Doyle and dragged him through the bedroom door.

"Tony's still outside there with the crackroaches and he's not dead yet." Doyle said and tears filled his eyes. "The roaches are eating him alive."

Anita pulled him close and hugged him and then she burst into tears also.

CHAPTER 23

Yes, just like Doyle had said, Tony was still alive, but he was in a hell in which the flames were hungry insects.

The roaches had him. They were inside him; they were outside of him; they were the universe he existed in.

There were fat cockroaches inside of Tony's mouth, hurrying up and down his throat. Some of them eating his gums, while others took dumps on his tongue. He tasted and smelt them; smelt them in more ways than one, because the smaller ones were crawling in and out of his nostrils too. Some of the bugs had made their way down his windpipe and were now drowning in the blood that was filling up his lungs as their larger fellows shredded his lungs from the outside, so they could reach and eat his weakly beating heart.

These smaller roaches had made their way into Tony's ears too. They'd plugged his ears and he now heard nothing except the chittering of their trapped and squashed bodies as their mouthparts hungrily scraped over his eardrums.

Tony dreaded cockroaches. They were the one insect he couldn't stomach.

Once as a kid, he'd lost a new baseball down a storm drain, and while trying to retrieve the ball, he'd accidently stuck his hand into a nest of roaches. That day, the disturbed bugs had swarmed out of the drain and had run all over Tony's hand in a brown tide that seemed impossible to stem.

At one point the nasty cockroaches had covered his hand exactly like a living baseball mitt, and that hadn't been the worst of it: the little boy had been unable to brush them off of his hand because of that similarity. He'd been unable to yell for help too. For those few terrifying moments, the bugs actually were a baseball glove.

Since that day Tony had dreaded cockroaches. For him they were the worst insect on the planet. The mere sight of one made him cringe in an unmanly way.

And that was why, when he'd seen what had happened to his girlfriend Sharon, how the bugs had covered her like that, something vital had snapped inside of his mind.

And now that the bright-eyed roaches were covering him too, Tony was suddenly right back there in the past, feeling around in the storm drain for his lost baseball, only this time, that living and squirming brown glove had covered his entire body and there was nowhere he could run to escape from it.

It wanted him and it had him.

In short, his will to survive had been horrified out of existence.

With no defense because his hands were bound behind him, Tony groaned and squirmed in agony. The orange-eyed roaches were eating him alive and he was in the direst pain imaginable.

And oddly, these mutant cockroaches seemed delighted with Tony's pain. It made his flesh taste even sweeter to them.

CHAPTER 24

Something's wrong with my brain today for sure, Gary Bentley thought, and not for the first time since leaving home. *I left a perfectly good dinner and my loving wife to come sit out here in the woods, hunting for what?*

Gary was sitting on a strategically positioned tree stump somewhere in the woods south of the Sleepaway Campground parking lot. He'd chosen this place based on the location of the stripped animal carcasses he'd found earlier in the day, choosing a spot somewhere in the middle of the imaginary line that connected those locations.

So he sat there, hugging his shotgun, and trying to stave off boredom. One problem with keeping watch like this was he couldn't really use his cellphone, as the light would both attract insects to him (which would be a major bother tonight), and at the same time drive away animals from him, possibly including the very creature he was hunting for.

This was a lonely spot and a quiet spot and even the insects seemed to dislike it. And speaking of insects, so far Gary had not once smelt that odd odor that had lingered around most of the kill sites.

He'd been here for half an hour now, waiting and watching, but like he was now asking himself, waiting and watching for what?

All I have to go on are these pictures, and they don't tell me much, do they?

He tapped on the screen of his phone, unlocked it, and flipped through the pictures again. The same gruesome images of animals so completely torn to shreds that it seemed the killer animal had been enraged. Which was part of what was bothering Gary. An enraged animal could be rabid. Or . . . much more worrying . . . it could have stumbled on a few chunks of Agent Orange.

Yeah, yeah, but there's unlikely to be any Agent Orange around here now.

He studied the images again, and then shook his head. Then he squinted up through the tree cover and tried to catch sight of the moon floating between the clouds.

Nah, this makes no sense at all to me. I must be crazy thinking I'd catch anything other than a cold, by hanging around in the woods at night like this. I'd better call it a night right now and head back home to Charlotte. I can't keep ignoring her calls like I've been doing. Alright that's it. I'm outa here—

Gary got to his feet. And of course, as if it had been waiting for him to give up his search, that was exactly when he heard the gunshot. A single gunshot.

"What the hell was that?" he asked himself aloud.

The gun report had come from over on his left, which meant the west side of the campground. But it had also sounded like it was quite a distance away. This both confused and relieved him. It confused him because he couldn't figure out who was shooting what at this time of night. And it relieved him because, had the sound been closer by, he'd have worried that one of the campers had just shot another, as he was very near to the most popular camping sites.

The unexpected noise also angered Gary Bentley. This last was because it might mean he wasn't about heading home to dinner and bed like he'd planned.

He didn't immediately leave this spot however. He figured he'd wait here a few minutes longer, just in case the elusive killer animal showed up.

So, he sat back down and once more tried not to get bored.

But about three minutes later, Gary heard another gunshot, apparently coming from the same location.

Sighing and now quite certain he'd be even later getting home tonight than he'd initially thought, Gary got to his feet and headed over in the direction of the gunshots.

What the hell's happening over there?

He still wasn't overly alarmed. Whatever the ruckus was, it clearly wasn't a gunfight. Too much time had elapsed between the first and second gunshots for enemies to be shooting at each other.

CHAPTER 25

Over in the cabin, nothing had really changed. The roaches were still eating Tony and Sharon in the living room, and the other four humans were trapped in the bedroom. Melissa and Bobby were sitting on the bed, while Anita hugged Doyle by the bedroom window.

"Shit, man, none of this had to happen," Doyle angrily told Bobby after a while. "You should've listened to me, and we'd have all made it safely out of here. Tony and Sharon didn't have to die."

Bobby nodded. "Yeah, you're right. But how was I supposed to know earlier that you weren't shitting me?"

"Yeah," Melissa said. "Who the hell would ever have believed that tale of giant killer bugs if they hadn't seen them with their own eyes? We both just assumed you and Tony had planned to double-cross us."

She and her boyfriend both glared at Doyle, as if daring him to argue with them.

Doyle let it go. In different circumstances, he might have persisted, trying to make the pair see that they were wrong and he was right, but the way their eyes were glowing now, he didn't dare argue with them. Doing so would be suicidal, since Bobby and Melissa still had all the guns. He was relieved enough that the pair of them weren't acting crazy anymore, even though both were still twitching occasionally.

People are unpredictable for sure. Bobby first deserted Tony and then saved me from the roaches, all in the space of five minutes.

"I'm scared of those two," Anita whispered in his ear.

He squeezed her close. "Don't worry, babe," he whispered back just as cautiously. "Just, whatever you do, don't argue with them. Let them say whatever they want, and you and I will go along with them as far as possible. You gotta remember that neither Bobby nor Melissa are in a rational state of mind right now. They may look it, but you'll soon find out they aren't."

"Their eyes are fucking creepy."

Doyle nodded and then laughed.

"Hey, share the joke," Bobby said. I could use a laugh right now. It feels like spiders are crawling through my guts."

"Hold on." Doyle cautiously opened the bedroom door a crack and peeked out. "They're still out there."

He was disgusted by what he saw—bare skeleton feet in place of human feet, and blood-splattered cockroaches pacing about. There were fewer cockroaches visible now. Several more of them seemed to have burst open from overeating or too-rapid growth. Unfortunately, this trend didn't apply to the largest of the roaches, which, once they realized the bedroom door was now open, hurried in its direction, their huge orange eyes somehow giving Doyle the impression of hatred and anger as well as hunger.

He shut the door hurriedly, and looked at the others.

"They're still out there. Most of them anyway."

"Well, what did you expect?" Bobby asked. "Those fuckers have our Agent Orange and they know we want it back. They're gonna fight us to keep it."

Melissa didn't say anything, but she nodded her agreement to his words.

Doyle shook his head and pointed to the bedroom windows. "Listen, we've a chance to escape now. We should just climb out of the window and run."

"No," Melissa said. I don't agree with you. There'll be more waiting for us out there. Bobby already told you they don't want to share the Agent Orange with us; that's why the bastards are trying to kill us."

"Listen, I've already told you I still have your original stash in my lab. Let's just head out—"

"Nah," Bobby interrupted him. "What we should really do is call the damn cops to come save our asses."

Doyle gaped at him. "The police. You want us to call the fucking police?"

Bobby looked surprised and then pulled his cellphone out of his pants pocket. "Why not?" he asked, waving the phone at Doyle. "Law enforcement have weapons to spare. They'll be here in no time at all and then we'll be saved."

"Okay, dude," Doyle agreed. Assuming that you do call the police, what are you going to tell them is happening out here?"

After asking this question, Doyle watched Bobby think it over for a few seconds, and then Bobby sighed. "They ain't gonna believe that we're being menaced by giant killer cockroaches, are they?"

Doyle had to laugh at the other man's frustrated facial expression. "You didn't believe the same story earlier, did you?"

"Stop fucking reminding us of that!" Melissa howled loudly, aiming her (actually his) revolver at him. "I'm gonna shoot you next time you do. Shit, I want my damn Agent Orange!"

"Yeah," Bobby said in a dangerously calm voice.

"Everyone, wait a minute," Anita said. Then, without explaining, she left Doyle's side and hurried into the en suite bathroom.

"Hey, guys, get in here quick!" she screamed almost immediately afterward.

Everyone ran into the bathroom and found Anita shaking and pointing over towards at the bathroom window.

"Shit, they're outside the cabin too," Bobby said on seeing the huge cockroach that was trying to force its way into the house through the window. It wasn't having much success, however, because the window was only partially open and seemed to be stuck in that position, only permitting the roach's head, two of its legs, and half of its thorax through, while its abdomen wobbled outside in the air like a segmented brown balloon. But even considering that it was stuck, the huge roach was still a horrible sight, particularly since its head was almost completely covered in blood.

Bobby nodded to Doyle. "Come on."

"Shoot it," Melissa urged them in a scared voice.

"We can't," Bobby told her. "If we accidentally break the glass, the others will be able to get in easily."

He and Doyle stepped over to the raised window. Keeping well to the side of the orange-eyed roach, which increased its efforts to climb inside as they neared it, Bobby said, "We'll just close the window on it. That should cut it in two."

"Hey, push it outside first," Melissa said.

Bobby shook his head. "There's no way I'm putting my hand anywhere near its mouth parts." He nodded to Doyle. "Okay, on the count of three, we reach around it and pull the window down."

"That seems worse," Doyle said. "It can easily bend sideways and reach us."

Bobby scowled. "You got a better idea?" But he too saw what Doyle meant. The giant bug was now squirming violently in place, twisting and turning and trying to get to each of them in turn.

"Hold on for a moment," Anita said.

The others waited while she ran back out into the bedroom and returned holding a can. She hurried past Melissa, and standing right in front of the bug, sprayed it in the face from the can. The giant bug immediately began jerking and twitching and suddenly wrenched itself out of the window and fell away out of sight.

Once the roach was out of the way, Doyle wasted no time in grabbing the window handle and both closing the window and latching it shut.

"What the hell did you spray it with?" Bobby asked Anita.

"Hairspray."

They made their way back outside into the bedroom.

"Okay, so now we know the bugs are outside the house as well as inside," Doyle said. Then he kicked the wall. "Dammit, if there was just someone we could call who wouldn't assume this was a Saturday night prank. There has to be someone who'll believe us."

"Hey, hold on," Anita said. "I know someone we can call who will believe our story." Everyone turned to look at her. "Call Dr. Cole," she told Doyle. "She's certain to believe you."

Almost like punctuation, they all heard a loud thump on the bedroom door. This was followed by another, even louder thump.

"You better hurry up and make that phone call," Bobby said nervously. "I think the damn roaches are getting hungry out there."

Doyle hurriedly dialed Dr. Annabelle Cole's phone number. The phone rang and rang and rang. And then went to voicemail. A second and third attempt produced exactly the same outcome.

"She isn't picking up," Doyle said.

"Leave her a voice message," Bobby said.

Doyle was about to do so when what was so far the loudest noise of all came from behind the bedroom door. This time the noise was accompanied by a cracking sound.

"I don't think they can break the door down," Anita said worriedly. "But they may be able to eat their way through it."

"Well, if we can't call the cops or your doctor boss," Bobby said abruptly. "I've got a much better idea."

"I'm listening," Doyle said, with Anita nodding her nervous agreement.

"How much insecticide do you have in your ride?" Bobby asked.

The question was so unexpected that Doyle gaped at Bobby. "What?"

Bobby nodded. "Don't look so surprised. They're insects, aren't they? Insecticide is guaranteed to kill them all." He pointed over at the bedroom vanity, on which stood Anita's can of hairspray. "It *that* worked against them, they won't have any resistance against actual bug spray."

Doyle was stunned. *Now why didn't I think of that?*

"I bought four giant cans," he said. "I was gonna keep two in the lab and take two home."

"Great," Bobby said, with a broad grin that revealed cracks in his grip on reality. "That way there's a can for each of us. I'll just jump out of the window, head around to your car and fetch the insecticide cans. Then we can all kill the roaches."

"It might be better to all go; then we can just drive away from here," Anita said, with Doyle nodding his agreement. "We know for certain that there's some roaches outside the house now. Okay, so maybe there aren't that many of them. But if we're together we'd stand a better chance of fighting them off than Bobby alone will."

"Shut the fuck up, bitch, and listen to Bobby!" Melissa spat and then leapt down off the bed. Pointing her gun at Anita, she added: "We've already told you what's going on here. The roaches are trying to cheat us out of our crack and we aren't gonna let them get away with it."

Bobby nodded and also pointed his gun at Doyle. "Yeah, bro, this isn't about getting high any longer. It's about the principle of the thing. Honor among addicts. The roaches have the Agent Orange, but they won't share it so we can all get high together. So, what we're gonna do is teach those fucking bugs a lesson they'll never forget. Then we'll take the drugs from them."

"I don't think there's any drugs left in the cabin now," Doyle said. "I think—"

"Shut the fuck up!" Melissa said, jabbing her gun into his side. "I'm starting to like you less and less. And if I like you any less than I do now I might just kill you."

Doyle and Anita were herded over to the bed and told to sit on it. Bobby walked over to the bedroom vanity and grabbed up the can of hairspray. "Just some additional insurance," he told them.

"Is this the irrational behavior you were talking about?" Anita whispered to Doyle as Bobby prepared to jump out of the window.

Doyle nodded. "You ain't seen nothing yet. Just hope that once we're alone with Melissa, she doesn't suggest us catching and eating the roaches to get high."

Bobby kissed Melissa and then leapt out of the window.

Behind him, the cracking sound at the bedroom door was growing louder.

CHAPTER 26

They heard the thump of Bobby's feet landing on the grass outside the cabin and then running off around the side of the building.

"Now we wait," Melissa said, shutting the window behind him.

Doyle and Anita nodded at her.

Melissa had barely gotten the window latched again, when all of a sudden, they heard Bobby shouting.

"Hey, hey, get off me! Get off of me! Nooo! That hurts! Shit!" Then came a long howl, and a gunshot.

"Dammit!" Melissa yelped in shock and immediately opened the window back up again. Then she leaned out through the window and howled out into the darkness: "Hey, baby, are you okay!? Are you alright!?"

The only response was a long yell that sounded anything but human. Then there was silence.

Doyle and Anita had by now joined Melissa by the window. Together, they leaned outside and stared along the cabin's rear wall. There was no sign of Bobby back here, but they could all hear chittering sounds mixed with nasty wet noises coming from beyond the edge of the cabin on their right.

"I don't think he made it," Anita said. "Shit!"

"Go and help him, Doyle!" Melissa said. "Go and . . ."

"No, you go," Doyle said, and bending down, he grabbed Melissa by the ankles and tipped her out of the window. Melissa went sprawling. She hit the grass outside of the cabin headfirst and lay still.

"What the hell did you do that for?" Anita asked him, while pointing outside at Melissa, who was slowly coming too, sitting up on the grass and holding her head. She kept blinking her eyes as if she was stunned. "You've just put her in danger."

"She was annoying. And she was about to endanger *me*. Did you hear her say I should go fetch that meathead boyfriend of hers? The guy's clearly dead now."

"Well, go out and help her back inside. Now, while the bugs are still busy eating Bobby."

"You know, this may be the distraction we need," Doyle said. "Let's climb outside too, grab Melissa, and leave Dodge Town at full speed."

Anita nodded. "Okay, that's a very good—" Then she shrieked, "Look out!" and shoved Doyle out of the way.

Doyle had the briefest glimpse of Melissa sitting upright on the ground and aiming her gun at him before he went flying towards the bed.

Behind him he heard a gunshot.

Shit! He'd landed on the bed unharmed and immediately turned around.

Oh my God no! Anita stood there swaying, with a massive hole in the right side of her head out of which her brains dripped. She was clearly dead on her feet, but true to Agent-Orange-junkie overkills, that wasn't enough for her slayer.

Melissa kept shooting, and those additional shots totally dissolved Anita's head and also flung her back across the room and slammed her against the wall.

Doyle leapt off the bed and ran over to Anita's corpse, which had just slumped down the wall to collapse on the floor. Right next to him, the bedroom door seemed to be on the point of dissolving beneath an avalanche of mutated insects, but that seemed a minor concern to him now. The clear and present bug danger seemed a far-off thing.

In shock, Doyle crouched next to Anita, staring at her pulped head, and then turned to face the window again. Melissa was leaning in through the window, smirking at him.

"What the fuck is wrong with you, you crazy bitch!?" Doyle yelled at her, leaping to his feet and heading for her, heedless of the revolver she was aiming at him. "Why the hell did you kill Anita?"

"I was aiming at you, you double-crossing sonofabitch." Melissa's orange eyes were practically bulging out of her face now. "Now I know why you never got us our orange. You're working with the damn bugs. Well, I'm onto you now!"

That said, she pulled the trigger. Doyle was about to fling himself sideways, but the gun clicked empty.

Melissa spat inside the bedroom. "Fuck you, chemist. I'll deal with you after I check on Bobby."

Then she leaned back out of the window and headed off towards the right corner of the house, around which Bobby had earlier vanished.

"Come back . . ." Doyle began saying. Then he let her go and turned back towards Anita and the bedroom door, which now had a long vertical crack in its lower half.

This is fucking crazy, Doyle thought. *This whole situation is fucking crazy. And I'm the craziest person of all here, to have even imagined I could become a drug dealer without karma biting my ass at some point!*

Then he heard screaming outside and turned back to gape at the open window again.

He ran over to the window and saw that it was Melissa screaming. She was running towards him, with a terrified expression on her face. "Oh, God no!"

"Get in here quick!" he said, leaning out to help her back inside.

But she ran past him as if she didn't see him. A moment later he understood why she was so frightened. Two giant airborne cockroaches—each of them the size of his head, were flying after her; with their mouth parts clicking. The roaches flew past the temptingly-open bedroom window as if it wasn't there and followed Melissa as she ran out of sight around the left corner of the house.

"Maybe they have a thing for hot redheads," Doyle thought.

Doyle shut the window and sat down on the bed. He stared at Anita, and now tears of sorrow for her death filled his eyes.

Yeah, I was nuts to ever get involved in dealing drugs! If I had a gun with some bullets in it I'd blow my brains out before things get any crazier.

Across from him, the crack in the bedroom door slowly got longer and wider.

CHAPTER 27

Gary Bentley had been moving at a moderate pace towards the river when he heard the second set of gunshots. These gunshots were all close together in time.

There could be no doubt about it now. Someone was shooting at someone else.

Or maybe they're shooting at a bear. Picking out his way with his flashlight, Gary quickened up his pace, and hurried along the river bank beneath its canopy of trees.

He'd already gotten out his cellphone to call for police backup. But then, realizing that the shooting had once again stopped, he put his cellphone away again.

I'll go have a look first and see what's going on over there. Then I'll have a better idea what to tell the 9-1-1 operator. Besides, the campers are likely to have already called the cops about the gunfire anyway.

Before this fresh round of shooting had erupted, Gary had already had a good idea of where the trouble was occurring. The new gunshots simply confirmed his opinion of that location.

The shooting has to be happening at that old cabin, the one near the new bridge the city just built to connect the upper and lower camping trails.

He'd reached the bridge now, and as he stepped up onto its wooden walkway, he could clearly see the cabin in question.

Well, the cabin lights are on, so there's definitely someone . . . Hey, who's this?

Someone was staggering towards the bridge. Gary swung the beam of his flashlight to cover the person just as they stepped onto the bridge.

It was a young woman. A young redhead who also just happened to be holding a gun. Most likely she was the one who'd been shooting.

She looked hurt, was swaying from side to side as if she'd drop to the ground at any minute. Gary couldn't immediately see what was wrong with her, but his flashlight revealed a long trail of blood behind her. However, she didn't seem to have been shot.

"Hey, miss, are you alright?" he asked, walking cautiously towards her. He instinctively raised his shotgun as she approached, though her own gun was down by her side and she showed no sign of raising it to point at him.

Then he played his flashlight over her face again and saw that her eyes were bright orange in color.

Oh, shit! he thought in dismay. *It's Agent Orange again.*

The girl seemed to notice him for the first time then, because she stopped moving forward and stood swaying from side to side like she was stoned.

"I heard gunshots," Gary said. "What's going on at the cabin?"

"This is all that asshole Doyle's fault," the redhead replied. "I hope the bastard rots in hell forever and ever."

And then she fell forward on her face and lay still.

Gary hurried over and crouched by her side. "Hey, miss . . . miss . . . mi—"

He leapt back up to his feet and shone his flashlight down at her body. Now it struck him that she wasn't just fainted, she was dead. And he could see why she'd died and why she'd been leaving that trail of blood.

Two huge bugs were buried in the redhead's back. Gary at first thought he was mistaken, that maybe they weren't insects, but animals. But no, he wasn't wrong.

There were two huge—*Are those cockroaches? They sure as hell look like it*—half-buried in the young woman's body, one on each side of her spinal cord.

The bug on the left side seemed to have tunneled its way up through her lungs to her heart, because, as Gary watched in horror, a thick jet of blood exploded outward from beneath the woman's ribcage and painted the huge bug completely red. On this happening, the second bug (yes, the insect was clearly a giant cockroach, easily the size of Gary's head) immediately withdrew its own head from whichever portion of the girl it had been feasting on and tried to drink up the squirting blood.

Gary sighed on seeing that the huge roach had bright orange eyes. *Fuck, it's happened again!*

Fast as lightning, he walked around the dead girl, took careful aim at the feeding roaches with his shotgun and fired.

The bugs exploded into mush. The girl was clearly already dead, so Gary doubted that she'd mind the additional damage to her body from the shotgun blast.

Then, staring worriedly at the cabin, Gary got out his cellphone and called 9-1-1.

"9-1-1, what is the nature of your emergency?"

Gary explained as best he could. The operator at first thought he was a drunk pranking her, but he told her to check his park ranger credentials and send help quickly.

The operator wanted more details, but he told her to just "Get the boys in blue out here as fast as they can make it," and hung up.

Then, realizing that time was precious here, he ran over to the cabin, to try to keep a lid on things until the police arrived. From the operator's own initially amused reaction when he'd told her about the giant bugs, he had the feeling it would take the cops a while to get here anyway.

And, as far as Gary was concerned, an infestation of giant crack-addicted cockroaches was something that didn't bear thinking about.

CHAPTER 28

Trouble was waiting for Gary at the cabin. As if on guard duty, an even larger cockroach than those that had killed the young woman on the bridge, was sitting on the cabin's front porch. He shone his flashlight on the bug. It too had huge orange eyes, and most of its body was bloody.

Just how many people are inside this cabin? Gary wondered. *And more important, how many of them are still alive?*

"Hey, is anyone alive in there!?" he shouted, for the moment standing well away from the porch and its huge insect sentry.

In response to his query the giant roach headed for him. He was surprised by how fast it moved on its many legs. Had he been standing up on the porch with it, it would have covered the distance between them before he would have a chance to shoot it. But being on the ground gave him the advantage. The roach was clearly too big to fly, and even had difficulty descending the steps. While it was still trying to lower its bulk down from the topmost step to the second from the top, Gary took careful aim at its head and shot it. He didn't want to fire at its body—its carapace looked tough as Kevlar—and see the pellets bounce harmlessly off of it.

The roach's head burst into mush and its body rolled down the steps, all the way to the ground.

Gary stared at its monstrous remains for a moment, then bounded up the stairs.

Now or never, he thought, pushing the front door open.

His plan was simple: he'd have a quick look inside the house, and if it was too full of crackhead roaches, he'd hurry back to the bridge and wait there until the police arrived, which hopefully wouldn't be too long from now.

The front door opened easily enough and he stepped inside.

What in the hell happened in here?

The front room of the cabin was full of huge orange-eyed roaches. But all of them were dead. After looking warily up overhead, just in case roaches of this size could climb the walls and ceiling, Gary leaned back against the jamb of the entrance door and tried to make sense of what he was seeing.

The dead roaches fell into three clear categories. Firstly, there were those that had been squashed to death. Those were clearly identifiable, by the deep unnatural indentations in their carapace. Second were the bugs that had exploded from internal pressure. Some of this category of roaches had merely a single crack running down their bodies from head to abdomen, with their innards—completely orange innards—squeezing out from the cracks, while yet others had popped like popcorn—these were fully exploded outward and now had the entirety of their innards on one side of their remains and the opened-up shell and limbs on the other.

The third category of dead roaches seemed to have been killed by their fellows. In all of these cases, the dead bug was upside down, and was missing quite a lot of its thorax and abdomen. Over by the corner, one such bug was still kicking its legs, though it no longer had a head.

Then, Gary realized that what he'd earlier mistaken for a large roach was actually a human head. He strode through the roach mess and had a closer look.

Yes, it was a woman's head, solely identifiable as female by the length of her hair, as all the skin of her face had been eaten off. Of her body he could see no trace, though he did see a single uneaten foot poking out from underneath the couch.

He grabbed hold of the foot and pulled. After some resistance as if it was stuck, the foot came free. A few seconds later, a cockroach emerged after the morsel to retrieve it.

This time Gary didn't waste ammo shooting the bug. Instead, once its body was sufficently out from under the couch, he stomped on it. He instantly regretted doing so, because it really exploded, squirting goop all over his boot.

Well, this room seems clean enough, he thought, after peeking beneath the couch and confirming that that had been the sole living bug in the living room.

"Hey, is there anyone alive in here!?" he shouted. "I'm park ranger Gary Bentley and I'm here to help you!"

"I'm alive," a weak male voice replied him. "I'm in the bedroom."

Gary hurried down the short hallway, towards the door from which the reply had come.

For a moment, standing outside the bedroom door, he didn't feel like going in there.

Something just ain't right about this.

He knew this because, even though the young man behind the door had replied him, the door was damaged. The door itself was shut, but its bottom half was shattered, leaving a massive archway which would easily grant the roaches access into the room. And if the roaches had managed to enter the room; how was the young man in there still alive?

Shit, I should just've remained home with Charlotte tonight. I also wish the boys in blue would hurry up! This ain't the situation I wanna be in right now.

Gary finally pushed the door open.

Gary winced. There were two people in the bedroom. One of them was dead, a young woman with fatal head trauma. She looked like she'd been shot in the head several times, and dumped against the wall.

The other person in the room wasn't dead yet; but surely soon would be. This was a young man sitting on the floor by the bedroom window, which was partly open. Obviously, he'd fallen down there while trying to escape the bedroom. Whether or not he'd killed the girl, Gary had no way of knowing.

The young man may have been trying to get away from the bugs, but he wouldn't be going anywhere now. He no longer had any arms or legs.

How the bugs had managed to sever his limbs without killing him, Gary knew he'd never work out. But somehow, they had. What they'd done with his limbs was however obvious. Four giant bugs sat there around the young man, who himself was propped up against the wall. Each of these four giant cockroaches was eating one of his severed limbs. Little of each limb was left uneaten.

Worse yet, the young man was blind, both of his eyes were missing.

Worst of all, a medium-sized cockroach was perched on the kid's head and was digging its mouth parts into his brain.

With blood streaming down his face from the violent intrusion into his brain, the blinded young man smiled creepily.

"Hello, ranger!" he said. "The bugs think I'm some kind of God. They're trying to get the secret of making Agent Orange out of me. They want it so bad, so so bad!"

After saying this, he began tittering like he was insane.

"Are you Doyle?" Gary asked the kid.

"Yeah, I'm Doyle," the kid replied, "and believe it or not, this is all my fucking fault."

And then, just like the young woman out on the bridge, he died. The armless and legless young man opened his mouth and vomited a lot of blood and then he stopped moving.

Gary sighed. Another unnecessary drug-related death.

Then he noticed that now that Doyle was dead, the four king-sized bugs were all dropping their remaining chunks of the kid's arms and legs and turning towards him.

Gary had had enough experience with crack-addicted animals to deduce what they were thinking.

"Sorry, guys, but I've no idea how to make Agent Orange and I've no fucking intention of learning how to," he told them.

He began shooting. Taking careful aim (and hoping he had enough ammo in the shotgun), he blew all four of the giant roaches to pieces, splattering bits of them all over the bedroom and over the corpse of Doyle, their last victim. The bugs chittered and skittered, but died one and all.

Then Gary's gun clicked empty. But he still had one bug left to deal with—the one that had been digging away in Doyle's brain. The bug was still poking into Doyle's brain, but now it seemed intent on tunneling down inside his head to hide itself.

"Fair enough," Gary said grimly. Then, unclipping his flashlight from his belt again, he walked forward and bashed the roach to pieces where it sat on Doyle's head.

Then Gary got the hell out of the bedroom and out of the house and went to wait by the bridge for law enforcement to show up. He doubted there were any more live crackroaches in the cabin, but he knew it would be stupid of him to do any more investigating in there when he was all out of shotgun ammo.

And, just like he'd suspected from the attitude of the 9-1-1 woman, law enforcement did take their sweet time with getting here.

No matter, Gary thought, as he waited. *I've one hell of a crazy tale to tell Charlotte tonight when I finally do get back home.* He laughed. *Maybe she won't stay mad at me for more than a week this time.*

The End.

ABOUT THE AUTHOR

Gary Lee Vincent was born in Clarksburg, West Virginia and is an accomplished author, musician, actor, producer, director and entrepreneur. In 2010, his horror novel *Darkened Hills* was selected as 2010 Book of the Year winner by *Foreword Reviews Magazine* and became the pilot novel for *DARKENED - THE WEST VIRGINIA VAMPIRE SERIES*, that encompasses the novels *Darkened Hills, Darkened Hollows, Darkened Waters, Darkened Souls, Darkened Minds* and *Darkened Destinies*.

He has also authored the bizarro thriller *Passageway*, a tribute to H.P. Lovecraft, *When the Bedposts Shake*, an erotic horror, *THE BLACK CIRCLE CHRONICLES*, a five-part mini-series that includes the books *Prove Your Love, Strange New Powers, Night Wings, Sheep Amongst Wolves*, and *Lord of the Birds*, and the *CRACKIMALS* series of horror-comedies (featuring titles *Crackcoon, Crackodile, Cracksquatch, Crackroaches, Crackadillo*, and *Crackaroo*) in association with Director Brad Twigg and screenwriter Todd Martin of Fuzzy Monkey Films, who is doing their film counterparts.

Gary co-authored the novel *Belly Timber* with John Russo, Solon Tsangaras, Dustin Kay and Ken Wallace, and co-authored the novel *Attack of the Melonheads* with Bob Gray and Solon Tsangaras.

As an actor, Gary has appeared in over a hundred feature films, including *Prove Your Love, Faded Memories, Midnight,* and *My Uncle John is a Zombie,* and multiple television series, including *House of Cards, Mindhunter, The Walking Dead,* and *Stranger Things.* You can also find Gary in the motion picture adaptation of *Crackcoon,* playing Jonathan, the forest ranger.

As a director, Gary got his directorial debut with *A Promise to Astrid.* He has also directed the films *Desk Clerk, Dispatched, Midnight, Godsend, Strange Friends,* and *Shoulder Down: Road to Redemption.*

OTHER GREAT TITLES FROM

WWW.BURNINGBULBPUBLISHING.COM

GARY LEE VINCENT

PASSAGEWAY

IMPOUND

GARY LEE VINCENT

GARY LEE VINCENT'S
DARKENED
THE WEST VIRGINIA VAMPIRE SERIES

DARKENED HILLS

When evil descends on a small West Virginia town, who will survive?

Jonathan did not start out his life to become a rambler, it just worked out that way. William was a troubled youth with something to hide. Both were from Melas, a small town tucked away in the West Virginia hills... a town where disappearances are happening more and more frequently.

After the suicide of a wanted serial killer, the townsfolk thought the nightmare was over. But when a centuries-old vampire is discovered they find out the hard way it's just getting started. Dark secrets can only stay hidden for so long and when the devil comes to collect, there will be hell to pay. Can Jonathan and William find a way to stop the vampire before it's too late? Find out in *Darkened Hills!*

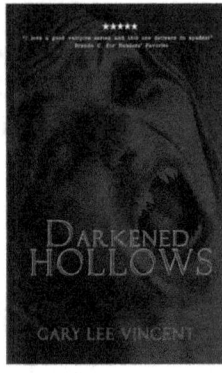

DARKENED HOLLOWS

In the heart-stopping sequel to the award-winning *Darkened Hills,* Jonathan and William must return to West Virginia to face possible criminal charges stemming from their last visit to the damned town of Melas, where both had narrowly escaped the clutches of a vampire seethe.

And as livestock start mysteriously getting murdered with all of their blood drained, worried farmers are searching for answers - leaving the local Sheriff and his deputy racing against time to learn the cause before a more violent crime is committed.

Burning Bulb
PUBLISHING

WWW.DARKENEDHILLS.COM

GARY LEE VINCENT'S
DARKENED
THE WEST VIRGINIA VAMPIRE SERIES

DARKENED WATERS

When the world goes to hell, the chosen must arise!

As Talman Cane orchestrates a flood of epic proportions in this third installment of the *Darkened* series the towns of Melas and Tarklin are caught completely off guard by the deluge. Hell-bent on finishing what they started, the evil brothers return to the lunatic asylum to take care of the witnesses and add to the ever-growing army of the undead.

Aided by Lucifer himself and the insane vampire demon Legion, the stage is set to channel all of the forces of hell to come forth. In an all-out race to survive, Jonathan, William, and Amanda soon discover they are up against impossible odds as Lucifer opens the Gateway to Hell, ushering in the zombie apocalypse and the End Times.

Find out who will survive this cosmic battle of the ages in *Darkened Waters!*

DARKENED SOULS

Melas and the Madison House are about to be rebuilt.
True evil is about to be reborne!

Young ex-priest and vampire-killer William is drawn back to the West Virginian town that almost killed him, where his vampire arch-enemy Victor Rothenstein still stalks the earth.

The town of Melas lies destroyed after the battle of the End of Days. But why is wealthy Jackie Nixon so eager to rebuild it using the bone dust of murdered souls?

Terrible evil has visited before, but the Gateway to Hell is about to be reopened in a horrific climax. And this time – it's personal.

WWW.DARKENEDHILLS.COM

GARY LEE VINCENT'S
DARKENED
THE WEST VIRGINIA VAMPIRE SERIES

DARKENED MINDS

Jackie Nixon intends to become Vampire Queen, but at what blood-drenched cost?

In this continuation to the explosive infernal saga begun in Darkened Souls, newly-turned vampire Jackie Nixon is taking no prisoners. Accompanied by her daughter, Kate, and by the captive vampire lord Victor Rothenstein, Jackie Nixon explores the Darkness. There, she intends to rouse the slumbering vampire race, bound under an ancient curse, and with their help, rule the human world.

But there's a deadly threat to Jackie's plans. Not just William who is trying to stop her, but her own royal ambitions. If Jackie performs the ritual to wake the sleeping vampires the wrong way, she could instead free the Red Beast of Hell, an unspeakable evil that even the undead fear.

DARKENED DESTINIES

With over 45 people missing after Jackie Nixon's party, the mysteries surrounding Melas and the Madison House keep getting darker.

Now, with legions of vampires at her command, can anything or anyone stop her from gaining complete control over all mankind?

The final battle has begun! As the Vampire Queen ascends her throne and sets to unleash the full forces of darkness, the fate of all things good hangs in the balance.

Burning Bulb
PUBLISHING

WWW.DARKENEDHILLS.COM

WHEN THE BEDPOSTS SHAKE

An Erotic Terror

GARY LEE VINCENT

STRANGE
FRIENDS

GARY LEE VINCENT

PROVE YOUR LOVE

GARY LEE VINCENT

STRANGE NEW
POWERS

THE BLACK CIRCLE CHRONICLES - BOOK 2

GARY LEE VINCENT

NIGHT WINGS

THE BLACK CIRCLE CHRONICLES - BOOK 3

GARY LEE VINCENT

SHEEP AMONGST
WOLVES

THE BLACK CIRCLE CHRONICLES - BOOK 4

GARY LEE VINCENT

LORD OF THE
BIRDS
THE BLACK CIRCLE CHRONICLES - BOOK 5
GARY LEE VINCENT

From the Creator of DARKENED HILLS...

RIVER
A VAMPIRE'S NIGHTMARE

GARY LEE VINCENT

A Vampire's Nightmare Continues . . .

RIVER

BOOK 2 ICARUS

GARY LEE VINCENT

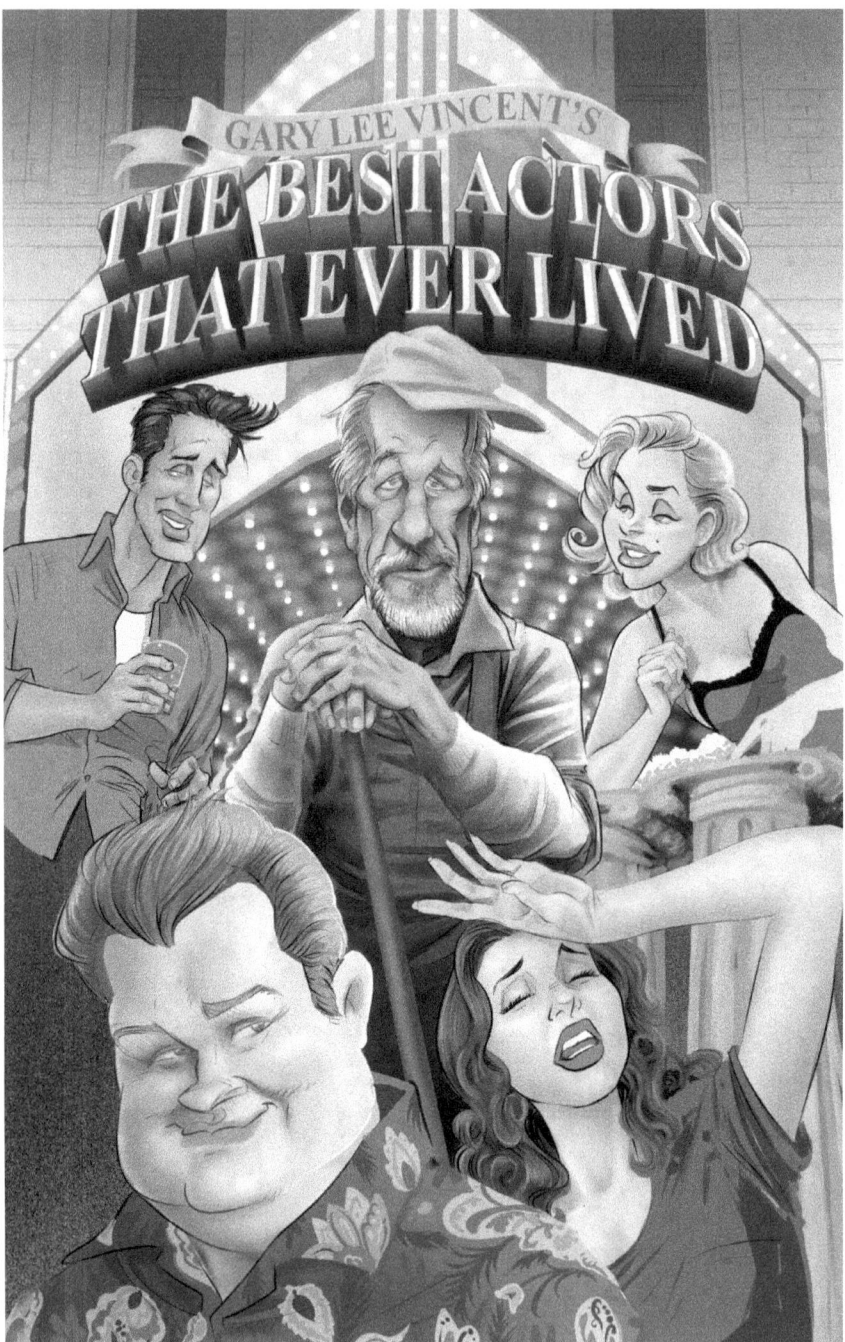

JEROME

A GHOST STORY

GARY LEE VINCENT

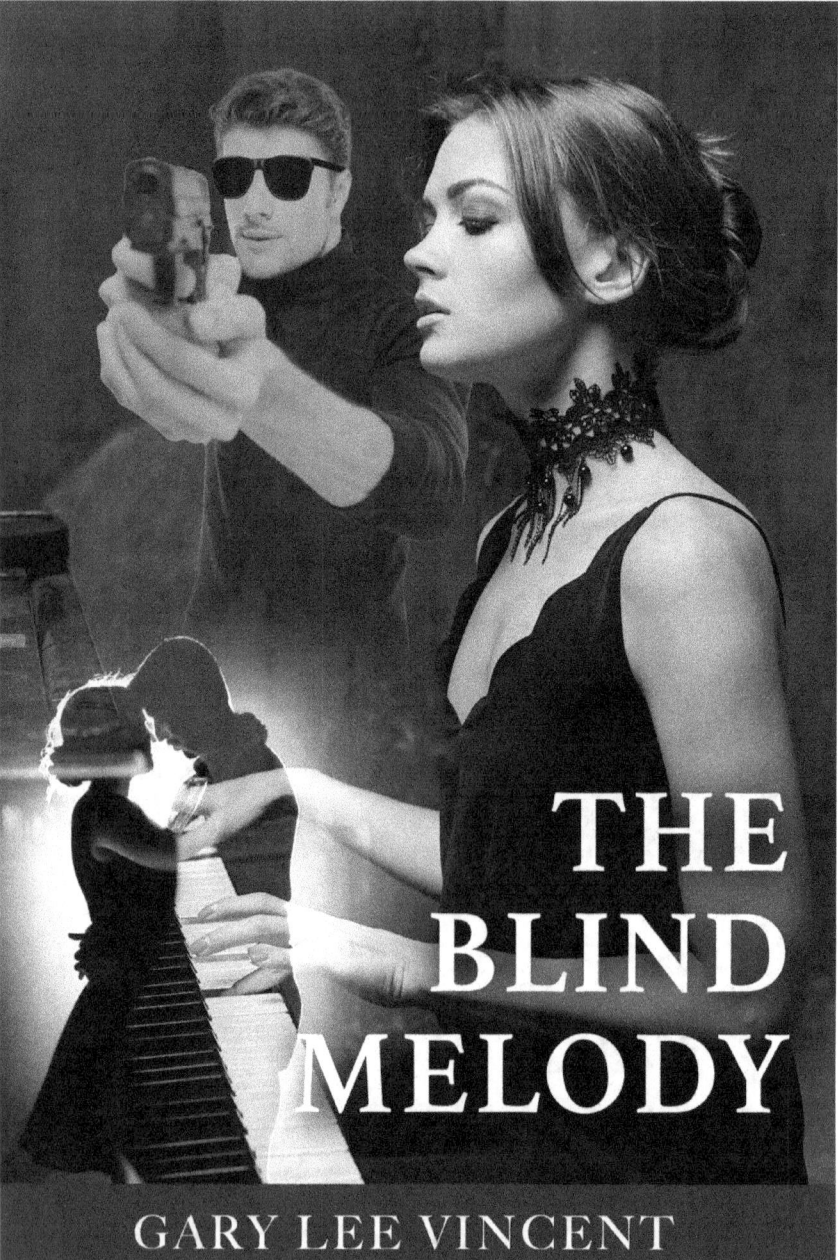

THE
BLIND
MELODY

GARY LEE VINCENT

RISE OF THE DEAD

AN EARTH-SHATTERING ANTHOLOGY OF ZOMBIE TERROR

Featuring Stories By:

John A. Russo   Tyson Blue   E.L. Stice   Nelson W. Pyles

Andy Rausch   Stephen Spignesi   R.D. Riley   Zakary McGaha

David J. Fairhead   Gary Lee Vincent   David C. Hayes   Rachel Montgomery

Paul Victor Wargelin   David F. Walker   William Vitka

Rich Bottles Jr.   Douglas Brode

www.ingramcontent.com/pod-product-compliance
Lightning Source LLC
Chambersburg PA
CBHW070939250626

47159CB00009B/3316